MARY

ADRIFT IN THE SEA OF SORROW

KATE CUNNINGHAM

READING RIDDLE

For Mum
Who infected me with book-fever at a young and
impressionable age

'There she is, the kidnapped woman.'

Mary Mallon
Known as Typhoid Mary
1909

Her world was white.

The shiny white of the table and the rough white of the floor. Shades of white on the tiny threads of her cotton clothes, and the crinkled white of the suits worn by all the Testers that came into her room.

She knew that the samples that came out of her were not white, but they took them away. Sometimes she wondered if everything was still white when the lights went out.

She thought not.

White was the only true colour.

It was as if her life were an empty canvas, waiting to be filled in.

2

Today was the day.

Vander had been working at the Charris Facility for six months now as a low-grade technician, and he longed to do more than constantly logging and testing samples. It had taken three years of training and banal, menial jobs, but his patience had finally paid off. There would be no processing today. In fifteen minutes, he was being trusted to go in and collect the samples.

Even the preparation had taken longer than he'd thought he could bear, and been exhaustive to the point of tedium. He certainly knew the drill inside out from endless repetition and had lost count of how many times he had practised stripping to his underwear, putting on the bio suit, opening the door and showering in the suit before giving the final door a lingering look and reversing the routine. Today was the first time he got to go through that door. Today it was real.

Normally, he had a steady hand, but now, when he most needed to remain collected, his fingers shook as he took a large gulp of coffee. It scalded his mouth and splashed on his white coat. It was outrageously wasteful, but he tipped the rest away before it did more damage and revealed his nerves. It wouldn't take much for them to change their minds and declare him unfit to be in charge of a syringe.

To calm himself, he went to the observation screen for one final look at the room and its occupant, both so tantalisingly near now. Mary was typically still. There wasn't much to look at, really. A young-looking teenager sitting on a chair in a basic white room. It was a similar size to his bedroom in the communal blocks where he lived, but a whole lot cleaner and much, much whiter. Clinical. It was hard to believe that someone so small was the source of so many specimens.

'That's her, then.'

Vander glanced at his older colleague. He had been a few years ahead of him at the training centre and, like him, had grown up in the Girin Child Bank. All the staff had come from there originally, but he remembered this one. He had always had a heartless self-interest. You were his friend until he got a better deal.

'Not much to look at, eh?'

Although it was exactly what he'd been thinking, Vander felt that the comment was crass, but not having anything to counteract it, he didn't reply.

His companion pressed on, keen to demonstrate that he had more experience than Vander. 'She looks like a girl, but she's not. She's a blank.'

Vander knew if he rose to the bait and got angry, he might lose this opportunity to go in. He took a deep breath. 'I know.'

'It messes with your head. The way she looks, and how you think she'll be. You can't know that until you go into that room. I'm just saying. She walks; she talks; but there's nothing in there. The lights are on, but nobody's home, if you know what I mean.'

Vander was annoyed by this need to state again what had been drummed into him since day one. But worse, he didn't really understand *why* this idea annoyed him so much. And he was annoyed that his older colleague could see he was annoyed.

'Of course, she wasn't always like that.'

Despite his irritation, Vander's curiosity was piqued. 'What do you mean?'

His colleague looked smug, and Vander rubbed his tongue on the roof of his sore mouth to stop himself snapping out a smart response. He shrugged to show he wasn't going to beg for the information and went to turn.

As expected, his colleague was not ready to lose his audience yet. 'At the start, they thought they'd throw in a few extra tests for good measure – test for intellectual impact, not just the biological stuff.'

Vander allowed himself to raise an eyebrow, aware a comment would expose his desperation to know more.

His colleague pressed on, impressed by his own authority. 'She learned to talk, was given regular cognitive tests. It's all logged. If you make it through the probationary period, you might get to read the reports.'

'So why did it stop?'

'Got too wily. Tried to convince a member of staff to take her home. Nearly succeeded. When it didn't happen, she got violent. Had to be suppressed with a chemical cocktail. Totally screwed up the testing for several years and set back the primary focus. They learned from that. Took her back to the beginning. A blank.'

They both looked at the girl again.

Vander was glad he no longer had the scalding coffee in his hand. Throwing it over his colleague would definitely have cancelled his session.

He turned away to get ready. His mood would be less obvious once he was changed, as no one could see him properly in his bio suit, and besides, it was time.

It was considered essential to maintain Mary's rigid routine. Nutrition at the same time, samples taken on the dot, and lights out at eight o'clock without fail. A regular little machine. Except she was a blank, not a machine, which meant that she had flesh, and blood, which he needed to draw out with a needle.

They had practised on each other in training; now it was time to do it for real.

He tried to focus on his preparations rather than his anger, going through the motions of dressing. Once he was done, he walked the final steps for the first time. He held his arm against the pad, and it registered the chip under his skin and released the catch. The door swung open and he stepped inside. He heard it close behind him. Mary did not move, but he felt that she was watching him without making it obvious.

She's a blank, he told himself. *You're making this a bigger deal than it is.*

He crossed to the hatch in the wall to collect the tray of syringes, which he carried over and placed on her table. As he reached for her arm, she shifted away. Vander thought of the observers and how they were assessing him, so, quietly fuming, he reached again, took her arm and tied the tourniquet before she could move again.

Mary was curious about this new Tester. She could sense that he was younger, more nervous, less distant.

'Stay still, please, Mary.'

Of course, the 'just a little scratch' still hurt, but she thought maybe he *cared* that it hurt, which most of them didn't. He tried to be gentle with the needle despite her little game.

As he reached to adjust the tourniquet on her arm before taking another sample, she turned to move it further out of reach again so he had to lean closer to her.

She put a hand out and touched the table. 'What colour is this?'

Vander nearly dropped the needle in his hand.

He knew she had functional speech, but this was more human than he'd expected.

No one had briefed him on the protocol for actual conversational interaction. His chest tightened, and he found himself taking shallow, fast breaths, making his visor begin to steam up. What should he do? Ignore her? Interact?

'What colour is the table?'

It was hard to hear her through the suit, as it was not designed for communicating. However, she seemed used to speaking loudly and clearly.

Vander cleared his throat. 'White.'

'What colour is this?' She spoke as if talking to a slow toddler and touched her suit in an exaggerated gesture.

Vander became aware that he was probably causing a stir behind the monitors. His first contact with the main research, and he was messing it up. 'White.'

'But they are not the same.' She held her unrolled sleeve over the table to show him. 'They are different.'

'Well, I guess one is brighter than the other,' he muttered.

'Brighter?'

'Sharper, cleaner.'

She let him draw the blood sample while she thought about this.

He was already pulling away, reaching out to gather the equipment and trying to leave.

She could not explain why she did what she did next. She never touched the Testers. They touched, prodded, poked and hurt her all the time, but she did not respond. As the Tester stood, she jumped up and grabbed his helmet in both hands. She pulled until her nose was against the visor and she could see his face inside. His mouth and eyes were open wide. His eyes. His eyes … were not white. A bit around the outside was, and there was dark in the middle. But around the dark …

He was gently pushing her away.

'Is there a problem?' The voice blared from the speaker by the electronic eye up in the ceiling.

'I'm just leaving.'

'Is there a problem?'

Mary released his helmet and moved away.

The Tester turned to the electronic eye. 'No problem. I'm just coming out.'

'Your eyes. What colour are your eyes?'

He bent to gather up the tourniquet, which had come loose and fallen on the floor.

'Blue.'

'Are my eyes blue?'

'No.' Big creases appeared across his forehead. 'Your eyes are green.' And then he turned quickly and was gone.

Vander was really rattled. As he showered and shed his bio suit, his mind was racing. She was a blank. A *blank*. But she hadn't seemed that blank to him. He concentrated as he

7

stepped through into the second changing area and quickly dressed in his lab clothes. His supervisor pounced on him as soon as he opened the door to leave the clearing room.

'What was that all about?'

'What?'

'The head holding. What did she do?'

Vander forced himself to sound casual and in control. 'You saw. She grabbed me.'

'And?'

'And nothing. She let go.' Vander looked away, trying not to look his supervisor in the face.

'She said something,' the supervisor pressed.

'You were listening in.'

'She took us by surprise. We heard the questions about the table and clothes. She's obsessed with colour. But she said something very quietly. We didn't catch it. What did she say?'

'Nothing important.'

The supervisor looked hard at the young man in front of him. 'You are new. You don't get to decide what is important. This isn't a game, and you are not working alone. What we do here could save us all from another plague.'

'I know.'

'So don't agitate the blank.'

Vander looked up angrily. 'I didn't do anything. You never told me she talks like that.'

The supervisor shook his head in exasperation. 'Of course she talks. How can she tell us about how she's feeling, otherwise? Complete your report and write down anything, *anything*, the blank says or does other than sit, shit or sleep. The three Ss. Do you understand?'

'Yes. I understand.'

'So go and do it now while you remember.'

Vander went back to the lab and pulled out a report sheet and a pen. There was no point in denying she had grabbed him. He stopped and remembered those green eyes as they stared into his.

Report 1 by Vander Girin-Charris

He paused as he looked at his name on paper. What had his name been before he was deposited at the Girin Child Bank? They didn't keep those records, as far as he knew. Occasionally a child was old enough to remember a birth name when they arrived, but it was soon taken away from them. They were now owned by Girin, and his indenture had been sold on to Charris. His brother might know, but then, they hadn't spoken for several years.

On entering the room, MARY seemed calm. I took one sample. At this point, MARY asked me to name the colour of the table. I told her it was white. She asked me to name the colour of her suit. I told her it was white.

I took the second sample.

MARY grabbed my helmet with both hands. She did not attempt to remove it.

VANDER HESITATED. Had she been trying to get it off? Had she been trying to hurt him? Vander remembered what Goff had told him. She hadn't pulled; she had just been looking. He thought about her other questions. If she was a blank, how would it occur to her to ask these kinds of questions? If she wasn't a blank ...? A shiver ran up his spine. They knew she had said something, but not what it was.

MARY repeated that the table was white. She released me, and I left the room.

HE LOOKED AT HIS HANDWRITING, at his lie. A little white lie. Why did it matter what she'd said to him? It meant nothing, but somehow it seemed personal and embarrassing to share.

He signed it, added a date and took it to his supervisor.

4

That night, as Vander lay on his thin mattress in the Facility hostel, he thought of Mary as he drifted close to sleep.

Her look haunted him. It was an expression he had seen hundreds of times before, not in the Facility, but in the Child Bank. It was the face a child wore when their parents had abandoned them, either through death or neglect, or simply through an inability to cope with a human other than themselves.

He'd probably looked exactly like that the night his father had deposited him there.

He remembered little of his life before the Bank. A few memories stuck out, pointy and sharp, painfully cutting through the fabric of their daily survival. The sharpest and pointiest of them all was his only real recollection of his mother as she lay sick and dying. She could hardly speak through the fever, and the unrelenting sound was of his younger brother crying in the other room, unattended and hungry.

He'd stood by her bedside with his father – his stepfather. They'd both watched helplessly as she'd struggled to

12

communicate her last thoughts, gripping the soaking sheets as if by clinging to them she could stay a little longer.

'Don't put them in the Bank,' she'd gasped again and again. 'Promise me. Free. Not the Bank.' His father had promised. He'd promised.

Of course, once she'd gone, his father had taken him there – not immediately, but soon enough. Not his brother. He'd kept him.

Vander had become an indentured member of the Girin Child Bank and had to fend for himself as he grew up. They'd paid for his food and a roof over his head, which had to be paid back. Like all other deposits, he had sold his contract on to a workplace, and so now the Facility owned him until he paid off the debt.

'I'll come and get you as soon as I can,' his father had promised. That promise had clearly meant as much to him as the one to his mother on her deathbed.

Later he'd realised they all said that to ease their consciences. But none of them ever did return. The longer they stayed, the bigger the debt, the less likely a relative would ever afford to pay it off.

He would never be free.

All his earnings at the Facility went towards the debt, but simultaneously a new debt was building for his food and lodgings here. In five years, ten years, fifteen years, he would still be lying on the same mildewed mattress, smelling the same stink of boiled food.

He definitely would never be free.

He'd wanted to kill his father for his broken promise. He still wanted to, but it was too late, because his father was already dead.

5

B   lue. Green. She closed her eyes and tried to hold
     blue in her mind. Blue like the new Tester's eyes.
     Green? What was green?

She dreamed of blue as she lay on her white bed in the dark that night. She would look at the Tester's blue eyes tomorrow and get him to explain green.

The next day, it was a different, older Tester, who kept a slight distance and refused to answer any questions about anything. She didn't want to look at his eyes anyway, and she was not sorry when he took his samples and left quickly. But as the days went by, she decided that either the blue Tester did not want to come back, or he was not allowed. After nine days, she stopped looking or hoping. Testers arrived, stuck needles in her and went away again.

She stopped moving. She wanted to sleep and dream of blue.

On the tenth day, the Tester came over to her bed to get the sample. She held out her arm without looking. This Tester was firm but gentle, taking her arm and scratching it with the needle. Instead of leaving immediately, the Tester moved so their back was towards the electronic eye, then took her hand, turned it and opened her fingers. A soft piece of cloth touched the palm of her hand, and quickly the Tester closed her fingers around it and returned her arm to the bed.

Quietly, so she could barely hear it, he whispered, 'This is green.'

She looked around quickly to see it was her blue Tester.

'Don't react, or they will take it.'

She wanted to grab him again, but he shook his head very slightly.

'My name is Vander,' he told her, and then he left.

Mary lay still on her bed for a long time. She turned so her body blocked her hand from the electronic eye, and without looking, she loosened her grip on the cloth, stroking it lightly with a finger. Slowly she opened the fingers and looked down to see green. She closed her hand around it again, afraid that the brightness of green would shine so brilliantly that the electronic eye would see it.

For a while, she held it and gave herself short bursts of green, until at last she turned her thoughts to how to hide it, how to keep her green safe. She had noticed that Vander had attached a metal clip at one end. Playing with it, she found one side moved and released a pin. It was like the puzzles that floated through her head sometimes. Memories or imaginings, she wasn't sure.

Moving gradually, she clipped it to the inside of her top. As she drifted off to sleep, Mary tried to remember if she had ever seen green in her dreams before. She could not remember, but now the night was full of green and blue and white.

In the following days, she watched carefully for Vander,

but again there was a gap between his visits that drained her energy and made her want to sleep. She trained herself to focus on him as she tipped into unconsciousness, to carry him with her into her dreams.

6

MARY *is experiencing a range of mood swings that vary between extreme happiness and despair, and manifest in some episodes of violent and aggressive behaviour.*

How old is she now?

> *She is sixteen, but her closed environment has delayed changes, and they haven't been obvious to this point.*

Is there any particular trigger, or do we think they are just hormonal changes?

> *There is a hormonal surge, nothing unexpected for a delayed adolescent. Nothing else particularly.*

Particularly? That suggests you have a thought. For goodness' sake, stop shilly-shallying and say everything so we can sort this out.

> *She had an episode where she interacted intimately with one of the new technicians.*

Intimately? What are we talking about?
Clarify.

She grabbed his mask and pushed her face against it.

And?

And that was all. The technician kept his cool and left. She
started appearing moody after that, but it's impossible to tell
if the incident was a trigger or part of something already
happening.

What is the technician like?

I don't understand.

You are employed to be observant. Old, young, tall, short, fat,
thin, covered in hair or warts?

Young, straight out of the academy. He is tall, fair. Very polite
and well spoken. He's originally from the Child Bank.

I see. It seems hormones can penetrate our biohazard suits.

Our suits are secure.

You really need to stop being so literal occasionally. Right.
Well, as you like the literal approach, add a hormonal profile
to all routine tests, and check it directly against the progress
of the microbe in her system.

Will this affect the progress of tests?

I don't know. That is why you are measuring it and looking for correlations. Anyway, we have a bigger problem.

We can counteract hormonal changes if necessary.

Indeed we can. However, the problem is more complex than that. Hormonal changes we can monitor and adjust. Emotional changes we cannot.

We could talk to her to assess her.

Not without giving her a lot more information and language to understand emotions and what they are. We tried that before, and it didn't end well. Arresting her development at five suited our purposes, but it seems we have been outflanked by adolescence. This one needs thinking about before reacting. Right. Go, go. Go and take samples and log results.

Is that all?

No. Deploy the fairest technician of them all to another sector for now, until we decide how to proceed with this.

All right. He keeps asking to be more involved with MARY. We could just terminate his contract.

No. We might find him useful in untangling this. Just move him and give him a line about extending his experience across the organisation. Don't tell him about any of this just yet.

7

Her days remained the same, but her green was slowly changing, with a small hole appearing in the middle where she rubbed it. The colour, too, was growing more like the darkness when the white went out. She had spent years with nothing to do, and it had seemed fine. She slept until the light came on. They stuck needles in her and gave her food. The dark came back. She slept. Again. And again. It used to be fine. But the arrival of this small bit of green had made it all seem unbearable.

To combat the boredom, she had begun testing herself to see if she could match the start of the dark by closing her eyes at the exact moment that it fell. Sometimes she just closed one eye to check if she had got it right; sometimes she opened them again immediately to check if it was now dark. Some days she couldn't be bothered. What did it matter whether it was light or dark? Who cared? She didn't think she did any more. On a good day, she was able to persuade herself that it was the act of closing her eyes that had made the dark happen, that she had control.

Now, when the dark started, she tried to direct her dreams to focus on green, but blue eyes floated into her vision. Vander. Immediately her pulse rate increased as he moved into her mind. After years of watching them measure the beat of her body, she could judge it accurately herself. She didn't need the machine to gauge how fast her heart was pumping.

She lay very still, listening to the rhythm, knowing it was different, but not sure why. She tested it. Imagining him never coming back again made it speed up and, bizarrely, made her eyes water. Remembering that moment with her face pressed to his visor made it faster to the point of pain.

Just as her heart began to slow, and sleep was finally coming, she was jolted back again by his voice. 'Mary, come with me.'

Although it was dark, he was there, pulling her up off the bed and briefly holding her close. 'Move quietly,' he whispered.

She staggered, still half-asleep, unsure whether this was real or not. Banging her knee hard against the table brought her round and fully into the present.

'Put this on, quickly.' He bent down and lifted a foot to guide it into the leg of a Tester bio suit and then repeated it with the other foot. She wobbled and grabbed hold of his back. Untangling himself from her grip, he guided her arms in and zipped her up. Just before he dropped the helmet over her head, he put his hands either side of her face and pulled it close to his visor so Mary was looking directly into his eyes.

'Follow close to me. Stay with me. I will explain every-thing later, but now we have to be quick.' Vander did not have the same awareness of his own heart rate, but he knew that it felt as if it were going to burst out of his chest, and it sounded far too loud. The drum of his heartbeat hammered in his ears and filled his helmet. If they had been in competition, he would have outstripped Mary's rate significantly.

As they reached the threshold of the room, Mary stopped suddenly, unsure what she was going to see outside the only space she had ever known.

Vander dragged her through the door. 'We're keeping these on for now. If we see anyone, they might not recognise you.' *But they may wonder why they were running around in bio suits*, he thought uneasily.

They went rapidly through two more sets of doors, and on the other side of the final doorway was a long, thin room that seemed to go on forever. At intervals along the wall were lights, flashing on and off. They were not white or blue or green. As Vander tried to hurry Mary along the corridor, she resisted, stopping by one of the lights to reach out and touch it. He stumbled, bumping into her as she blocked him. He followed her gaze.

'What is it? It's not green.'

'Red. It's red. Come, Mary. Come with me, and I will show you all the colours.' His mouth stretched, and a sound came out.

'What are you doing?'

'I'm laughing. Come on.' He gently coaxed her along the room. And she felt it inside her, a bubbling, uncontrollable feeling racing around her body, giving her energy. A sound came out and she laughed too, and it felt amazing.

The walls seemed to go on forever, but they finally reached the far end, and Vander took his arm and held it against an electronic access pad. A huge door slid open, leading to the black void outside the building. Mary gasped at the endlessness of it and felt as if she were tilting forward, unable to stand upright as the ground seemed to shift. She grabbed Vander to stop herself falling. He hustled her through the doorway and slammed it shut behind them. They staggered along the outer wall and collapsed in a heap. He lifted off Mary's helmet and gently pushed her head between her knees.

'Take long, slow breaths. We are outside. I should have thought. I never stopped to think about how this would make you feel.' He rubbed her back gently, and gradually the spinning feeling slowed down.

'I realise you feel bad, Mary, but if we don't go quickly, you will be put back in the room again, and you will never have another chance to see anything else. I can show you purple, pink, yellow, orange.' He waved his hand around. 'I can show you anything you want out here. But if you go back, I can't show you anything, and they won't let me see you again.'

He sat down in front of her. All the strength and energy had drained from her now the red had gone. She reached out and touched his hair.

'Come on. I can't believe their security was that rubbish. They never thought anyone would want to get you out, so we've taken them by surprise, but they'll find us soon unless we keep moving.'

He held out his hand to take hers and led her over to some trees. She felt numb but let him gently strip off the suit, reversing the process they had gone through back inside.

Vander pulled out a dark bag and started bringing out clothes, which he handed over.

'Can you try and put these on?'

She nodded and attempted to balance and insert her limbs into the correct parts, with Vander occasionally leaning across and guiding her.

'These are trousers. They're blue, a dark blue. A lot of

people wear them, so you'll not stand out so much. I had to guess your size, but they look okay. Let's just do up the button ... Now for the top. Just a hoodie for now. It's a bit big. We'll have to get you something else, but this is different, so we're not running around in the Facility suits like convicts. I wanted to get you a bright jumper with lots of colours, but we have to blend in for now. Later, maybe.' He stopped to stretch his mouth again, but this time, no sound came out.

Mary reached out to touch his lips. 'Are you laughing again?'

'No. This is smiling. Same movement and sort of feeling, but not so ...'

'Not so ...?' She found she was doing the same action.

'Nearly there. Socks and shoes.'

'They're hard. I don't like them.' She started to try to pull them off her feet again, but Vander pushed her hand away.

'The ground is sometimes sharp. They'll protect your feet.' He laughed as he watched her take her first steps in the shoes, lifting her feet high above the ground so they didn't drag with their heaviness.

'Just walk normally, or they'll spot you.' He had taken off his suit and was already wearing other clothes underneath.

'I'm trying to, but this is different. It's hard.'

'Don't think about it; just run.'

He grabbed her hand and headed into the trees.

Strange things filled her nose, sharp, powerful aromas so different from the normal smell of her room, so many overpowering smells that she had no words for and that threatened to suffocate her.

They came to a wall of wire.

'Here. I cut a gap already. You'll have to crawl through.'

This was so easy. Vander could not believe he'd just walked Mary out of the Facility without being stopped. Flip a switch, and the audible alarm system turned off; walk out the door. Nothing was this easy. Was it? Where were the security guards or the dogs? Was no one watching all the fancy monitors?

There was only one more thing to do. The Facility expected Mary to stay put, but they clearly didn't put the same trust in their staff. Like all his colleagues, he had a security chip that identified him, gave him access to the Facility and carried his medical records for easy access, 'just in case'. He didn't know how far the chip transmitted, but he needed to ditch it too in case it allowed them to track him. Unfortunately, it was under the skin of his upper arm. Quickly, he ran his hands down Mary's arms to check she didn't have one too. As he'd thought, there was no hard strip that he could feel.

'Don't look,' he instructed her. Then, gritting his teeth, he made a cut over the chip. Gagging, he stuck small tweezers into the gash. The long, thin shard did not come out easily, and the blood was making it more slippery.

'Let me.' Mary took over and surprisingly quickly pulled it out and threw it to the ground. She looked at him. 'I know quite a lot about needles, blood and cuts.'

He passed her a pad and bandage from the bag, and she bound it tightly.

'You could have been taking your own samples all this time.'

She shrugged. 'Probably. It was usually good to see someone else. Otherwise, I wouldn't have met you, and anyway, no one ever asked me to.'

Vander took a swig from a bottle in the bag. A little whisky to dull the pain.

'Can I have some? I'm thirsty.'

'No. It's knockout juice. Sorry. We'll get water back at the flat. Come on, we have a long way to go yet.'

8

What happened to the security?

    The security was working.

The security was not working.

    There were no breaks in the security.

Stop wasting my time with diversions and excuses. There was the most monumental breach in security. The thing being guarded got up and walked out last night, apparently with no difficulty at all. This was not an armed raid, no tunnels or helicopters, just someone with an access chip, a pair of wire cutters and a lot of balls. Am I missing something?

    No.

In fact, you are right. There was no break in security, as there appears to be no security at all.

Only employees have access chips, and they are subdermal inserts.

Is there tracking in them?

Yes, but the chip was cut out and left at the perimeter.

So we know whose chip was used.

Yes. It was the new tech that MARY reacted to.

I thought we – and by 'we', I mean you – were monitoring that situation.

We'd moved him. He had been thoroughly checked before we employed him. As previously mentioned, he was from your Child Bank. A model resident, deposited by his stepfather when he was eight, after his mother died in the last sweep of the Red Plague. His natural father was a scientist who died in the first wave. The boy showed a strong aptitude for the work. No one wants to come near this place. With the plague still active, no one wants to risk taking anything out of here.

But he did, it seems.

Our money goes into the scientific work, not pointless guns and security.

Well, there won't be a great deal of scientific work going on if we've lost our key participant. It would help to know what he hoped to achieve by this liberation. Maybe our little orphan tech wanted revenge on a world that robbed him of his parents. He has very little to lose.

Except his own life. I'd say that was a pretty big thing to risk losing.

But apparently, he doesn't agree with you. Please go away and use our funds to increase security, and then put together a briefing explaining exactly what we are going to do next.

You mean about getting MARY back?

Maybe. Actually, perhaps we have an opportunity here.

If we don't get her back, there's a very real risk that she'll start another wave of sickness.

Yes. I know.

So it is our priority.

Our priority is to keep the Facility operating, and recently there have been a lot of mutterings from the stakeholders that maybe we don't need the full grants from the other sections. Perhaps this is what they need – a reminder about how essential our work is.

We are talking about the survival of humans.

I don't think we need to let it get that far out of hand. Just a little localised outbreak in a poorer part of the city. Then we sweep her up and carry on, hopefully with some updated resources and a fuller appreciation of our importance. Excellent. Off you go and organise that.

9

Getting out had been easy. Getting away wasn't. Walking down the street with a traumatised girl was considerably more complex than turning off the alarm.

They had made it halfway to the flat that Vander had organised, and both of them were exhausted. It was not the distance but the sheer difficulty of making Mary move forward and keep moving. Vander realised that he'd seriously underestimated how emotionally painful this would be.

They'd run for a short while, but Mary had barely walked more than a couple of metres across a closed room before. They'd fallen into a slow marching step that was interrupted by frequent stops as a new sound or smell hit Mary full in the face. Each time she stopped and asked, 'What is that?' Vander was struck by his failure to notice the peaty tang of wet soil or the screech of an owl.

Their march was slowing to a walk, and now they stumbled along, with Mary almost paralysed by the sensory overload. Every sight, every smell, every sound was new and terrifying.

Vander had expected to be at the flat by now, and there hadn't been room in the bag for coats. The temperature had dropped dramatically, and the air was cold. Mary's hands felt like ice, and Vander had very little spare body heat to share. As the wind picked up, it blew her hair and caught her jacket, flapping it around. She screamed and tried to bring them back under control, looking around wildly to find what was attacking her.

'It's the air moving around.'

'Make it stop! Make it stop!' she cried.

'I can't. It just does it.' He drew her close to him to shield her a little, but now the heavens opened, and rain began to fall.

Mary stopped.

'Keep going.'

'I can't.'

'We have to.'

They'd finally reached the other side of the wooded area that surrounded the Facility and were coming to a small group of shops, which were closed and shuttered for the night. Vander pulled her towards a doorway. He had planned to walk the route and be back by now, but clearly, they weren't going to make it on foot. They were near the station, and soon the early trains would start running. Since the Red Plague had decimated the population, electrical power was only available between certain hours, and the trains might be busy, but perhaps that would hide them more effectively than if they were out on their own. Nevertheless, having seen how she was in what he thought would be the quiet part of the journey, he was anxious about her possible reactions to travelling on a train.

'Mary? Do you want to go back to the room?'

31

'Yes. Back to the room.' She nodded, thinking longingly of her familiar bed.

'No. No, you don't mean that.'

She began to whine. 'I want to go back. Take me back.'

Vander started to panic, and he angrily shook her, being rougher than he'd intended. 'You can't go back. You just can't. If you go back now, you will never be allowed to leave again. They won't allow it. You need to be brave. If you go back, I will be in really big trouble. They'll put me in a locked room too.' He took big breaths, trying to turn the tide of fear rising in him. 'Be brave for me.'

'I can't.'

'Then I'll take you back.'

'If we go back, will you stay with me?'

'If I take you back, you won't see me ever again. You will have to do all the walking we've already done to get back, and then I will have to leave you.'

'Why are you doing this to me?' Vander was unsure if her shout was to the sky or the rain or the Testers or him.

He pulled her close. He opened his jacket and made a tent around her, trying to block the sights and sounds out. Gently and quietly he made sounds to calm her, as if she were a scared animal. 'Shhhhh, shhh, shhh.'

Gradually, Mary relaxed a little.

'I know this is really hard. I know you're scared and overwhelmed. I know a big part of you wants to run back to the safety of the Facility. But, Mary, if you do, you will regret it. You'll end up being sorry. If you can be brave, I'll show you things that you can't imagine yet. This feels bad, but it will get better. If you go back, it will never get better and never get worse. It will be nothing. Forever. Do you understand what I'm saying? Mary?'

She was shaking uncontrollably. She was hyperventilating like a scared rabbit on the verge of a heart attack. He held her firmly and stroked and shushed her, drawing her back to the reality she was trying to face. Eventually, the shuddering became shivering, and finally it eased.

With her head against his chest, she could hear his heart thumping. She closed her eyes and felt their bodies synchronise. Slower. Slower. Slower. *Dum. Dum. Dum.*

'Yes. I understand.'

'What do you want to do?'

'You think I should carry on.'

'I do.'

She gripped his hand. 'Go on.'

Vander hugged her. 'Right. Let's try this.'

He pulled Mary's oversized hood further over her head and drew the cord tight so it now covered her ears and her eyes, and was firmly in place. He tucked her tightly between his body and arm, and wrapped his jacket around them both. Reaching across with his other hand, he checked that she wasn't suffocating.

'Trust me. Close your eyes, and I'll guide you.'

Slowly he walked towards the station. He hummed gently to try to further drown out the sounds around them.

'We're going into the station.' He knew the daytime schedule well but had never travelled in the early hours of the day. However, it seemed that finally their luck was back. A train was due, and now he needed to ensure Mary didn't panic during the next stage.

'Mary, there's going to be a very loud noise in a minute. It's just the train. It won't hurt you.'

Vander winced as the old train wheels grated on the tracks while it pulled up to the platform. He shivered at the name on the side of the carriage. Hownner Charris. Hownner ran the power supply, but Charris ran not only the transport system but also the medical supplies. He had just broken Mary out of the Charris Facility. He shook himself. He would become a nervous wreck if he fell apart every time he saw the name.

Hownnner, Charris, Danssy, Wuckenoge and Girin owned everything. The five wealthiest men at the time of the plague had hidden away in their bunkers, then swooped in to take control as the old order crumbled, floundered and failed to grasp the seriousness of the situation until it was too late. As the value of money tumbled they had grabbed the resources along with the loyalty of those who wanted to eat too.

Vander took a deep breath and focussed on what he needed to do to stop Mary shutting down, and himself from running away and hiding. To distract them, and pull them back together, Vander maintained a running commentary of every step. 'We're by the train door now. We're going to get on. Take a step up. We're inside, and we need to sit down, so we're going to back up, and here we are. Sit down here.'

He pulled her closer as they sat, wrapping his arms around her.

'It will move around a bit. It's okay,' he whispered. Then he closed his eyes to prevent himself from making eye contact with the other passengers and hummed gently to try to drown out the sound of the train.

As it set off, Mary tensed and made a small sound, but the rocking soon lulled her, and finally she became heavy with sleep. Vander struggled to stay awake so they did not miss their stop, nodding and jerking as he drifted in and out of wakefulness.

As the train arrived at their destination, Vander pulled Mary into his arms and managed to lift and carry her. She was slim and small, but the adrenaline had drained from him, and he staggered a little on stepping down onto the platform, and so he focused on moving forward one step at a time. Their destination was only a twenty-minute walk from the station in normal circumstances. However, before long he had to admit defeat and put her down. The last stretch felt as long as the rest of the journey put together.

They crossed the derelict land that surrounded the last remaining block of flats. Once, the whole area had been crammed with housing, but after it became clear how much of the population had died, a lot had been demolished. They had said it was a chance to destroy infected properties and build new, clean homes, but it seemed obvious that Jem Danssy, the Head of housing, meant to limit the remaining accommodation. The Heads of the various amenities had quickly realised that having control of the housing, farms, energy, medicine and orphaned workforce maintained their power base in a post-plague world.

Dawn was breaking as they arrived. There was no one around. Vander had selected it for its isolation and abandonment, but as the light grew, he knew it now made them more obvious. He was almost carrying Mary as she collapsed from lack of sleep and the mental and physical exhaustion from the night of slow travelling.

Even if they had got away without being seen, Mary's absence would soon be discovered when the lights came on at the Facility and the morning nutrition was delivered. If they'd already detected the escape, they would be hot on their heels.

Vander didn't register another occupant watching them as he looked out to see the sun rise over the cityscape. If Vander had noticed him, he probably wouldn't have cared as, with one final push of energy, he lifted Mary into his arms again for the last stint up the stairs to the third floor.

Arriving at the flat, he propped her against the wall and opened the door. There were only two rooms, and the second held a single bed. By now Vander would have slept anywhere, and Mary had already succumbed. After putting her down as gently as he could, he lay down next to her.

Grey light filtered through the ragged curtains, but for once Vander was spared naming it for her.

10

Barely two hours after they had collapsed onto the bed, there was a banging on the door. Vander lurched across the room, scraping his arm on the door frame.

'Who is it?'

'The guards coming to take you away, aha, oho.'

He opened the door and hauled the visitor inside. He was slightly taller and thinner than Vander, with wispy, uncombed hair and a patchy, half-formed beard.

'That's not funny, Scratch.'

His friend was unrepentant. 'What would have been very funny is if the Wuckers had knocked nicely on your door, rather than smashing it in and then bashing you about.'

'Really not funny.'

Vander stretched and sat on the wonky chair, running his fingers through his hair and rubbing his face.

'Did you do it?'

Vander jolted up to look at his friend. Scratch fidgeted and scratched, as he did when agitated or nervous. 'Yeah. I did it.'

'Well, you don't look overjoyed. Can I ask yet what it is you did?'

'Better not.'

Scratch stopped still for a moment and looked at Vander.

'Is this big trouble, or better still, big money, and if so, how come you want me to run around after you and won't let me in on the big secret?'

'There's no money in this, Scratch. I promise you, if there was, I'd cut you in.'

Vander took the bulging bag that Scratch had brought in and put it on the worktop. He walked over to the sink and was relieved when water spluttered out of the tap when turned. After filling a glass, he drank it down.

'There will be trouble, but I'm trying to keep you out of it by not telling you anything. I just need you to do a couple of shopping trips for us, and then we're away.'

Scratch pulled out a chair and sprawled across it. 'Who's "us"?'

Vander cursed his thoughtlessness and considered whether to tell Scratch some of the story.

'I'm helping someone out. I can't tell you, because it's not just my arse on the line.'

'Don't you trust me?'

'You're the only person I do trust. I just don't want to get you any more involved than I already have.'

'You can't stay here forever if they're looking for you. Where are you going to go?'

'I don't know.'

Vander could see Scratch was not convinced. It was stupid but true. He hadn't really believed they would get out so easily; he hadn't thought much past there. The only plan he had in place was to get Scratch to buy them some food if they made it to the flat. He'd staked out the building beforehand and checked which one still had some basic furniture and plates and cups. The trainees all got a meagre allowance for extras like underwear and soap, and he'd been carefully keeping a little back for emergencies. He reckoned this qualified as an emergency and he had given some to Scratch. Other than that, there was no plan.

'I just wanted to get this far. If you don't know anything, you can tell them that with a clear conscience. In a few days, we'll disappear, and hopefully, no one but you will even know we were here.'

'And Barb.'

'And Barb what?'

'And Barb knows you're here.'

Vander tried to stay calm and breathe deeply. He was good at hiding anger; it was partly what had got him the training to work at the Facility, his calm, rational approach to situations. Years of practice had paid off, and even his closest and only friend didn't see the slightest flicker of the rage as he wrestled to hold it tight inside him.

'Why did you tell Barb?'

'I don't really do shopping, Vander, so I had to get her to help me out. She was all for doing a runner with the money, so I had to tell her it was for you. She knew I wouldn't run off with your money.'

'So you told her that you were helping me out and you'd just pop the shopping round to me. Why did you have to tell her where I was?'

'Well, she insisted on coming with me. I don't think she actually trusts me that much, to be honest. She probably thought I had another girl somewhere.'

'So how does she know you aren't up here with another girl?'

39

'Yeah, could you just wave out the window to her, Vander? I was going to ask, but you've worked it all out yourself. You were always good like that.'

Vander hurried over to the window and peered out through the grime to the desolate square below. Most people kept well away from these blocks, as they were superstitious about old ghosts and fearful of lingering microbes. Rumours about the Heads probably circulated to keep them in line. However, Barb wasn't the kind of girl who believed in spirits or dirt. She didn't run from things but took them on with the full expectation of winning. She was pacing impatiently around the paved courtyard three floors below, kicking at the ground. She stopped to pick up a stone and throw it at something that scuttled through the shadows of the long-abandoned children's climbing frame.

'What's she doing out there? It looks really obvious something's going on with her hanging around like that.' Vander could hear the rising hysteria in his voice.

The careful calm was slipping away.

'Well. Truth is, she doesn't really like you that much. Sorry.'

Vander shrugged. He knew Barb didn't like him, and she knew he didn't like her. He suspected Scratch knew it too, but as in most relationships, it was sometimes easier to ignore bad feelings rather than confront them. There had always been a battle to control Scratch's affections since childhood, and it had sometimes escalated into immature taletelling. A deep uneasiness stirred in Vander. It had seemed okay to tell Scratch, but he hadn't considered sharing it with anyone who actively disliked him. It made the decision easier: they would be on the move as soon as possible. They wouldn't be staying any longer than they had to, and he wouldn't be sharing the details of their move with anyone this time.

He waved to Barb, and she threw back a contemptuous look and a rude gesture.

'What are you doing?'

Mary stood in the doorway. She looked blearily around the room. Vander strode across and put an arm around her protectively.

'I was just checking something.'

He looked across at Scratch, who inevitably was grinning and winking at him in what he seemed to think was a discreet way. Vander sighed. Scratch could insinuate all he liked; Mary wouldn't have a clue what he was trying to suggest, anyway.

'The big secret?'

'Sort of.' *If only it were so simple*, Vander thought.

'My tongue is dry and my stomach hurts.' Mary touched her stomach, looking alarmed as it growled.

It was her first experience of hunger and thirst.

'You just need some of this food I brought you.' Scratch was fishing for gratitude, but Vander wasn't in the mood, and Mary didn't understand. 'Good breakfast'll set you right.'

Mary opened her mouth to ask for an explanation, but Vander headed her off.

'I'll explain later. You need water and nutrition. Here.' He sat her down on a chair opposite Scratch and got a glass of water for her. He filled the glass that he had marked with an M when he'd prepared the flat. He was fully aware that out of the biohazard suits, precautions were probably pointless, but not sharing body fluids had seemed a sensible idea.

As she drank, he turned to empty the bag Scratch had brought with him.

It seemed Barb could follow a shopping list even if Scratch couldn't. He was pretty sure there should have been some credit from the shop, but it was probably fair to give them that for doing it and not just running off with all the money. Barb would certainly think so.

He hadn't been sure what Mary would eat other than the Facility slop, but thought it best to start off with something bland. He gave her a slice of bread to at least keep the rumbles at bay while he sorted the rest out.

Vander's head hurt from trying to settle Mary and not alert Scratch to where she had come from. 'Shouldn't you be going? Barb will be getting impatient.'

'Hmm. She'll be all right for a bit. Hi. I'm Scratch. I'm Vander's friend.'

Mary looked up from studying the bread.

'I got you that food.'

Vander was almost tempted to observe how this attempt at charm went, but as he already knew it was doomed to failure and miscommunication, he crossed to the window again to check what Barb was doing. He couldn't see her, and uneasily he thought it unlikely she had gone home without Scratch. He could do without her seeing Mary.

'Scratch, I think Barb is getting lonely down there. You ought to go and find her and check she's all right.'

'I could bring her up to meet your friend. It would be like a double date.'

Vander swung around to say what he thought of that idea when he saw the glass marked *M* in Scratch's hand.

'What are you doing?'

'I was thirsty. It's a long way up those stairs.'

The residual calm was gone, and Vander could hardly breathe as the anger choked him. 'That's Mary's glass. Give it back to her.'

'I was just borrowing it.' Scratch threw back his head and drained the last of the water from the cup.

Vander threw his arms over his head and felt the roaring building up inside him. 'Get out. Get out now.'

'All right. What's your problem?'

'You need to leave.'

Scratch looked at Mary in a meaningful way that was completely lost on her. 'Someone needs a little more sleep, I think.'

He walked to the door. 'You've got to chill out a bit, Vander. I think you're getting too stressed out. Do you want me to come back in a couple of days and check on you?'

Vander nodded, afraid to say anything, anxiously watching to see if Scratch made it to the door without collapsing or foaming at the mouth. All he could do was see if his friend came back in a couple of days. He suppressed the tiny voice that wanted to know if he'd make it that long, if all those precautions at the Facility had been necessary or were just one big game.

As he left, Scratch turned.

'Well. Goodbye, mystery girl who seems to be driving my friend a little crazy.' The hint to give any further information having failed, he turned.

Vander slammed the door and leaned on it, with his ear to the crack.

'No. Come on, we're leaving. He's got some girl in there. You ask me, he's lost it a bit ... Yeah, I've still got the credit. I told you he wouldn't push for it.'

The footsteps faded as they travelled down the stairwell, and they were gone.

He turned and looked at Mary, who seemed completely unmoved by the event.

'How do I get all this in my mouth?' She was still holding the whole slice.

Vander started to speak but then stopped in open-mouthed amazement as Mary took the bread, and watching him carefully for his reaction, stuffed it into her mouth, padding out her cheeks like a hamster.

'You're meant to break it up and eat it bit by bit.' He offered her another glass of water and stepped back as she opened her mouth, allowing half-chewed bread to fall out.

'I'm going to cook us something a bit more interesting than bread.' He sorted through the shopping, picking out the knobbly vegetables and a stock cube. 'I'll make some soup, I think. That'll stop your stomach grumbling.'

He felt Mary come up behind him.

'What's soup?'

She had no sense of personal space and leaned against him as she looked at the food on the counter. She still had the slightly acidic smell that had pervaded the Facility, but it was fading now, and it was mixed with a muskier, more human scent. In the mucky surroundings of the flat, she looked out of place, too perfect and unmarked.

'Is it this?' She held up a carrot and looked at him, pleased to have identified the soup.

'No, but it will be,' he said, taking it off her. 'I'll show you.'

11

'Is this where you've always lived?'

Vander came away from the curtain, where he had been standing most of the afternoon.

'No. This is just for us, just for a short time. I lived at the Child Bank with Scratch and a load of other kids.'

'Lots of you all together?'

'Yeah. Never a moment's peace or quiet.'

Mary tried to imagine it, but she had never met anyone younger than the Testers, who were generally a lot older than Vander.

'Can we go there?'

Vander hesitated. It had crossed his mind that it would be a good place to go. Mary could have disappeared among the mass of strange kids that lived there. For the most part, they would have accepted her and not questioned her unusual behaviour. Often the older kids that turned up on the doorstep, or who were handed in, had lived odd lives surviving outside the system.

He thought of Caz, who had said she was fifteen but looked ten years older. She had turned up with three younger siblings. They'd been living off old, tinned food and the rubbish from the dustbins around the back of the academies, where the Heads trained their staff. Most scavengers worked that way, but the stashes of old, preserved food were almost impossible to find now. The younger kids had adapted to the Child Bank lifestyle and embraced the regular meals, but Caz had disappeared one night after being caught too many times trying to break into Matron's store cupboard.

No one had been quite clear whether she had chosen to leave or been taken by the Wuckers, who kept a vague sense of order under the most feared Head.

Barb had been one of those later arrivals. Before that he and Scratch had been inseparable, but she'd made a beeline for Scratch and stuck to him from the moment she'd arrived. She'd been brought in and left by her family, smallholders who no longer grew enough food to feed all the mouths. They'd chosen Barb to dump, although Vander had heard her tell Scratch that she had younger siblings that they could have chosen instead. But they'd chosen her. She'd never said why, at least not when he could hear.

The new arrivals were almost always hungry, withdrawn and often anti-social. They all latched on to Scratch to start with, but they always found their own place and group of friends, and moved on. All except Barb, who had stuck to Scratch like a thorn in Vander's side.

He looked up and saw that Mary was still expecting an answer to her suggestion.

'It might not be safe there. The Facility will be looking for you, and there's lots of germs among all those kids. I thought you might get ill from them.'

It was true that Mary's immune system was probably very limited. It was lucky that excuse had just popped into his head.

Of course, there was also the small matter of how infectious Mary might be. How infectious was she? It didn't seem like a good idea to find out in a large building filled with children. Better for her to stay here with him. A much safer option all round.

He tried hard not to think about Scratch's exposure to her earlier, or that he was back at the Bank right now.

Deep in the back of his mind sat the uncomfortable knowledge that he was not about to share Mary with the heaving masses of the Child Bank. It wasn't just food you had to compete for within those walls; you had to compete for every scrap of human affection and love. Vander had no illusion that he would win such a battle if pitted against some of the more outgoing characters. He could care for her perfectly well here, and it was so much simpler without the extra emotional conflict. He pushed away the disturbing thought that kept trying to derail him, that this position made him not much better than the Facility.

12

Barb first noticed something wrong when they went to get off the train. It suddenly occurred to her that Scratch had hardly spoken a word the whole journey. She didn't normally talk to him, but he did talk at her the whole time in a continuous stream of one-sided conversation. She just tended to zone out and carry on with her thoughts.

Today she'd been considering how to organise a mass bed-changing rota. There had been a surge of bedbugs through the rooms, and they were all being bitten to death. If they made a competition of it, they could try to clear them all out at once rather than chasing them from one room to another and back again. This should have been Matron's job, but frankly, she neither cared nor could be bothered. She was more than happy to let Barb organise it, and take credit afterwards. In fairness, she would ensure they had all the things they needed: insect powders, detergent, cleaning equipment. She just wouldn't organise it or take part in it.

The arrangement suited them both. Barb liked to straighten things out and make them right; Matron liked to have an easy life. It also meant that neither Scratch nor Barb would be allocated a job and moved out. They were both past the age when most of the banked children were sent to train in one of the academies run by the Heads. Depending on their strength, intelligence and skills, they might be chosen to work in the power factories or sent out to the farmlands. Some were trained to work on the transport. Others mended houses, or the particularly mean ones ended up as Wuckers, keeping a basic level of order among the young population.

They were indentured posts: once you started, there was no getting out, because you had to pay for all the resources that had gone into keeping you at the Child Bank. At the peak of the plague, as all the previous social structures had collapsed, the reins of power had been gathered up by the Heads, who had got together and split up the roles. Brandon Charris ran transport and medicine; Jem Danssy was in charge of agriculture and housing; Job Hownner had responsibility for the power grid; and Gareth Wuckenoge enforced security and the law. Of course, their own Leo Girin took on the Child Bank. They fed and housed you, but in return, your labour belonged to them, until you could no longer work. There were rumours that once you couldn't work, you were disposed of. With the workforce still quite young, that hadn't really been considered yet.

Barb guessed that, unofficially, she and Scratch had been allocated as assisting in the running of the Child Bank, which suited her. She was happy to make it all work, but as always, Scratch was essential to her plans. She could tell the kids what to do; Scratch would make it exciting and get them actually doing it. A couple of hundred children, babies to teenagers, would daunt most normal people, but Scratch just saw it as an enormous bunch of friends.

She smiled as she imagined him lining them up with brushes and buckets, pretending they were an army going to war against the bugs: *Line up, soldiers! Hold that brush straight! Ready? Quick march! Come on, give it your all. You don't want to end up like me, all scratching all the time.*

They reached their stop, and they rose unsteadily. She looked at him carefully as he dropped out of the carriage and started to walk towards the Child Bank. His steps were an uneven stagger instead of his usual long, steady lope. He stumbled over a rough patch and seemed a little disorientated. He'd always been a slow walker, so it was hard to tell the difference, but she'd walked alongside him for many years and could tell he wasn't right.

Looking up into his face, she could see beads of sweat along his top lip, touching the fuzz of his developing facial hair. She took his hand and squeezed it, and he turned a little and gave a smile in return.

As they entered the grounds around the Bank, her worst fears were confirmed. The little kids mobbed him to play games and join them, but he brushed them gently away and headed to his room. Scratch never ever turned down the chance to play with the littlies. However dopey or tired he was, he always had time to play, talk, listen and care for them. This churning mass of damaged and lonely children could have been a place of nightmares, but it wasn't, because Scratch loved them all.

She pulled them off him. 'Come on, kiddies. Scratch isn't well. Give him his space.' But she did it kindly, knowing what their Scratch time meant to them – a pocket of kindness in a cruel world. Goodness knows they got little enough happiness as it was.

Barb guided him to the stairs, and they started to climb up to their room on the sixth floor. This used to be an old hospital. Once the plague had swept through the patients and then the rest of the population, it had been cleared and left empty. Girin had taken it over for the Child Bank – it was convenient with large wards and kitchens and cleaning areas. She guessed at some point it had been thoroughly disinfected after the apocalyptic scenes at the height of the Red Plague, but it didn't do to think about these things too much. None of the younger children had even a vague memory of that time; for them, it was ancient history. She and Scratch had a room in what used to be the private area, where the spaces were smaller, with their own bathroom and only one bed.

As they slowly ascended the stairs, travelling up the building, the overriding smell changed from urine on the lower levels to sweat and smelly feet the higher they got. It reflected the natural progress the kids all made, from the maternity wards if they entered as babies, through the various levels going upwards as they matured into their teen years, to the top, where the rooms were smaller and had better views across what used to be a park but now was more like a wooded heath.

Unfortunately, being at the top meant more climbing and more effort, which usually wasn't a problem. But today it was slow progress. There were lifts, but they had stopped working reliably long ago, and they kept the younger children out by telling them the shaft was full of cockroaches that lived in the dark, oily pit at the bottom and climbed the walls with their sticky feet. For all she knew, it was true; she wasn't going to check it out any time soon.

Finally, she got Scratch to the top and onto their bed. On the last flight of stairs, he had needed to lean on her, and her ear was pressed against his chest as she propped him up. She could clearly hear the wheezing of each breath as it went in, and the rattling as it escaped out again. Although he was thin, he was considerably taller than Barb, and it had exhausted her getting there. Luckily, one of his more persistent followers had shadowed them up the stairs and now peered around the corner of their door.

'Go and get Matron,' Barb called to her. 'Tell her Scratch is ill. She needs to come.'

The girl spun around and raced off down the stairs. She was clingy but reliable and would get Matron up here somehow.

Matron's room was on the ground floor. She said it was to check the entrance and watch the grounds, but everyone knew she was lazy and almost never came up the stairs if she could help it. So it was a surprise when Barb heard her coming, wheezing even more loudly than Scratch had done.

'Why didn't you bring him to me downstairs?' she complained as she came in the room.

'I wanted to get him into bed. Anyway, he wasn't as bad as this at the bottom.' Barb took his hand, which was cold and clammy, even though his face was red and sweating. His eyes were closed, and his breathing was now fast and shallow.

Matron took one look at him and started backing out of the door.

'Why did you bring him back here? Oh my God, what have you done?' She turned into the corridor and put a hand out to steady herself against the wall.

Barb glanced at Scratch and then chased after her. 'Come back and check him!' she shouted at Matron, but in return she shook her head.

'No, no, no, no, no.' Matron closed her eyes as if denying and blocking this would make it go away. Barb stepped forward and shook her arm, and Matron leapt away from her as if she had been burnt. 'Don't touch me! Get away! You've been touching him. Don't you touch me.'

'What is it? What's going on? You haven't even examined him.'

'I don't need to go any nearer, thank you,' Matron spat. 'He has the Red Plague, and you've brought it here. You have it now, and I've probably got it.' She moaned and rubbed her hands over her face. 'We're all going to die.'

Barb slapped her, and more quickly than she had ever moved before in her life, Matron slapped her back. 'You've killed us all.' And she turned to run down the stairs.

Barb thought of all the children downstairs crowding around Scratch as they had arrived back. It couldn't be the Red Plague. It had died down years ago; there weren't even any flare-ups now. She walked back into the room and took Scratch's hand, but although he was still breathing, he did not respond to her touch. How could he have got the plague?

She lay down next to him and put her arms around him. 'Scratch, you've got to fight this. Matron's wrong. There is no more Red Plague; you've just caught a nasty bug. Scratch, I need you. The kids need you.'

She rubbed her tears off on the pillow and whispered, though there was no one else in the room, 'Scratch, I love you.' She had never said those soppy words before, and she was shocked and scared that they had come out of her mouth now.

How could this have happened?

Then she remembered that Vander worked at the Facility. The place where strange things were meant to happen. No one in their right mind went near there or wanted to work there. Some said it was where the Red Plague had started in the first place, and everyone was sure it still had something to do with it. When she could leave Scratch, if he got better ... no, *when* he got better, she was going back to the flat where Vander was hiding out with his mystery woman, and she was going to kill him, if he wasn't dead already.

13

We've had word of an outbreak of the Red Plague at the Child Bank.

Ah, good.

Good?

Well, it's a lead, isn't it? If there is plague there, then it must be where they have gone. How did we hear about it?

Matron ran here as soon as she saw a case.

How noble of her.

She's in quarantine now. Sedated. She's a little hysterical.

Next steps?

Should we send in the Wuckers?

No.

No? They'll want to know.

I dare say they will, but not yet. Let's see what's happening, shall we?

I don't understand.

Send in a team with full bio cover to see what is happening there. Hopefully, they will find MARY, and they can bring her back and seal off the Child Bank.

We'll bring the ill children back.

I didn't say that.

But we need to isolate them from the healthy ones.

Not yet. They all had a dose of the latest experimental vaccination last month.

It doesn't seem to be working.

We don't know that yet. Retrieve MARY and seal it off. It's all terribly unfortunate, but out of misfortune comes opportunity. And this is our opportunity to see how our vaccination fares. Right, run along and get MARY back. Oh, and remember, no need to inform the other Heads just yet. Hopefully, we can brief them once we have good news about the inoculations.

Some might think you set this up.

Might they? Oh well, you can't help what others think.

14

Mary looked at the food on the plate in front of her.

'I don't like that.'

Vander looked at the food he had presented her with. It was true that it didn't look very appealing, but he wasn't much of a cook. In the Child Bank and the Facility, they had food provided, cooked en masse for them all. 'It's all we have.'

'I don't want it.'

Vander knew he should coax, or trick, or wheedle, but he didn't have the energy. He guessed it was all the exertion of the escape and the drop in adrenaline now they were here, but he felt absolutely wrung out.

'Just eat the food, Mary.'

'No.' The sweep of her hand took the plate and the meal onto the floor, where it ended as a mixed heap of broken crockery and potato.

Vander sat very still with his eyes closed and his fists clenched.

She can't help it. She can't help it, he chanted silently to himself.

When he opened his eyes, Mary was sitting silently on her chair as if back in the Facility. Vander forced himself to press down the pounding anger he felt surging through him, and finally he trusted himself to speak.

'It's okay to get mad, but you have to look at what happens and learn from it.' He realised that he sounded just like the patronising elders in the Child Bank when they talked to the younger children.

Her eyes moved to look at him, but nothing else moved.

He tried again. 'I don't think you meant to ruin your lunch, did you?'

There was a tiny shake of her head.

'You have to eat to stay strong, and we don't have much choice over what food we have. We only have the food that Scratch brought in the bag. Do you understand?'

Mary gave a tiny nod.

Vander got up and fetched his serving from the side. He put it in front of Mary, who hesitated, then began to eat. He hadn't diced this plateful yet, but she showed that she'd been watching with her clumsy attempts to cut it up herself.

Vander walked behind her chair, and leaning over, he put his hands over hers as she used the knife and fork. Adjusting her grip, he then guided them and helped her correctly angle and push the cutlery so it cut.

He felt a deep, protective warmth as he moved his hands over hers, but at the same time a bubble of resentment as he helped her eat his meal. 'If you do something wrong, you should say sorry.'

'Sorry.' It was automatic and meaningless, but she had said it.

As she finished, she turned to him. 'Where's your food?'

He pointed to the now-empty plate before her.

Realisation dawned. 'You gave me your food. But what will you eat?'

'It doesn't matter.'

Tears trickled down her face, and now Vander knew she really was sorry.

'It's done. Finished. No good crying over spilled milk.'

'I thought milk was that white water you gave me to drink.'

'It is. It's an expression. Something people say when things go wrong. It means it's too late to worry about.'

Mary sniffed. 'Why not just say that?'

'I've no idea. People usually understand. Come on, help me clean it up. I'll show you how.'

Vander got a brush and started to sweep up the mess on the floor, and Mary got a cloth down from the side. She had seen Vander wiping the table with it earlier, and now she got down on her hands and knees, and started rubbing the floor in circular motions, grinding the food into the floor.

'No, no. Stop. You're making it worse.' Vander snatched the cloth from her hand and glared at her. 'Just move out of the way and let me clear it.'

'I'm trying to help.'

'But you're not helping. Go and sit over there.'

'Like at the Facility. "Sit still and don't cause any problems."'

'This is not like the Facility – I just need you to let me clear up.' Vander turned away because he wanted to scream out or throw something, and the rage frightened him.

It had been a long time since he'd felt such pumping anger, and back then he'd climbed to the roof of the Child Bank and sat up there alone, imagining a better future. The intensity of the mood brought with it a flash of remembrance, of looking across the treetops, surveying the land beyond the confines of his prison walls. Which direction would he head in as soon as he was able to escape? Across the river to the farmlands to the south? No. Too wild. There was nothing for him there. His eyes crossed the land between the grey stripe of river and the rusty slash of the rail track, which marked the boundaries of where the majority of the population now lived in the remaining housing. Beyond the track lay the academies – that was where he was destined, but which one? A Wucker? No. Too soft. He was too soft, too unwilling to take orders. Not the Danssy building either – its concrete warehouse was the nearest and took the most children, but he had no desire to build or do manual work.

His eye was always finally drawn up the hills to the white roof of the Facility and the mysteries that lay within. That was where he would go, he'd decided. He was going to make his mark, and it would be therein that he would do it. This memory, this certainty, brought a sick feeling to the pit of his stomach.

Suddenly he was jolted back to the present and realised Mary was speaking.

'I didn't ask for this. I didn't make you take me out of the Facility. Why did you have to do that?'

'You were a prisoner. You were locked up, and I thought it was wrong. You seemed unhappy and confused.'

'I didn't even know what it meant to have those feelings.'

'You were asking questions that were impossible to answer without showing you. There was so much you didn't know. They were keeping it from you, and I wanted to show you. Maybe I shouldn't have bothered.'

'So you thought you were helping me?'

'Yes, of course. What do you mean by that? Of course it

was to help you. Do you think I thought I was going to get anything out of this?'

Vander pushed the chair over and stormed across the room.

'You have no idea what I've given up to do this for you. How dare you question why I did this! I did it for you.'

'Why are you angry with me? I don't understand.'

'You don't understand. You don't understand.' He threw his hands up in the air.

'No, I don't. I throw my food on the floor, and you sit calmly and give me yours without a word. I ask you why you're being nice to me, and you get really, really angry. I don't understand.'

'And I can't explain it.' He took a deep breath and set the chair upright again. He sat and put his head in his hands.

Mary came over and sat on the floor at Vander's feet. 'Why don't you try? I learn really quickly, and I want to know.' She put out her hand and rested it on his arm.

Vander sat up from his hunched position and threw his head back with a huge sigh. 'I got you out because it was wrong to keep you there like that, and I wanted to help. But also ... also, I got you out because I wanted ... I wanted ... a friend.'

'Friend?'

'Someone you like and spend time with. Someone who shares your ideas and who you have fun with. In the Child Bank, you share everything, and nothing is special. You follow the rules, and everything will be safe. You can't say what you think or question things. But you ... you question everything, and you would be mine ... my friend. My special person. I'm not explaining this right.' He thought of Barb and Scratch, and how they were together. They were the most unlikely couple: Barb so organised, confident and spiky, and Scratch so laid-back, friendly and silly. It was never ever said, not even by the craziest kids in the Bank, but they clearly loved each other.

Mary pulled on his arm. 'But that's okay. We can be friends.'

'No.' Vander stood up and paced around the room. He felt light-headed and a bit disorientated. 'It's more than that. It's all those things, but there is more too. I wanted a special kind of friendship. Friendship you get between adults, between grown-ups and ... and ...'

'And I'm not grown-up.'

'It's not your fault that you're not. You see everything like a child, and I'm like your parent. I didn't want to be a parent. I wanted ... I wanted something different.' Vander rubbed his face with both hands. 'I was so stupid.'

He returned to another seat and bowed his head. He watched the dust fly around his legs in angry whirlwinds that gradually slowed and settled.

'Are you sorry you got me out? You could go, and I'll look after myself.'

Vander snorted.

'I know I wouldn't do it very well, but I'd try. I'm not sorry you got me out. My life was just white, and now it's got lots of colours, and I want to find more, so I'm not going back. You are sorry, but I'm not.'

'I'm not sorry. It's just not what I expected. I'm disappointed and cross that I didn't see it. It's not your fault.'

'Well, it is, but I didn't do it on purpose. I'm changing. I'm getting better, and maybe one day we could be friends. I want to try.'

Vander felt strangely hot inside, but his skin was clammy. He knew that there was a fever slowly building in his body, and as a breath caught in his throat, he was sure he could feel the fluid rising in his lungs. He didn't know how long he had left. He'd thought it would be longer – he'd hoped it would be. Another thing he had failed to predict correctly.

'I'm trying, Vander. Don't give up.'

'Yes. You're right. It will work out.'

She came over and hugged him. 'You're cold. Come to bed. I'll warm you up.'

Vander smiled wryly to himself. *Vander, be strong*, he thought, and let Mary lead him to the bed to lie next to her.

Mary watched his muscles gradually soften as he moved towards sleep. It didn't come easily to him. He fought it, tossing and turning, then twitching and jerking. But finally he succumbed.

The light of the day was dimming already. Mary went to the window to watch the sun gradually go out instead of flicking off in one go. She pressed her fingers to her mouth to stop herself laughing out loud as it seemed to put on a display of colours especially for her.

She checked that Vander was really asleep, because he had already told her off for pulling the curtain back earlier. He was.

If she slipped in between the curtain and the window, she realised, it would be less obvious what she was doing.

The sky was a sort of smudged blue, but not all over. There were white patches, which looked a bit dirty. As the sky became darker, a pale red and yellowish colour appeared from nowhere. Mary shook her head in frustration. There must be better words for this.

Looking down towards the courtyard, she froze as she realised that she was being watched. He looked surprised too as he stood staring at her in the window. He frowned and finally looked away before heading into the block.

Mary watched him go and felt an anxious knot in her stomach. She stood for a long time listening for footsteps or a knock at the door, but none came.

Should I wake Vander? He said not to open the curtains, but they weren't really open, were they? she justified to herself.

She knew she had done wrong, and she also knew that she wouldn't be telling Vander about it.

15

As twilight fell, Max was walking across the derelict land to his flat. He was tired after his shift at the train station, which had seemed busier than usual. It hadn't been much, but he was aware of small fluctuations, having only seen the same three people for the first seventeen years of his life. It was why he chose to live here, in the empty flats. After a day of processing new faces, he needed a break from the rest of the human race.

Walking slowly, he savoured being out, and being alone, which was when he looked up.

Initially he thought he was imagining it when he saw a person at the window of that flat. He was even more certain he was hallucinating when he scrunched up his eyes to focus and saw a beautiful young woman. She looked incredibly pale, ghostlike. Her eyes were big, and she had short hair. She looked so perfect, so much like an apparition, that he really might have written off the sighting as tiredness or wishful thinking if she hadn't looked so shocked on seeing him.

He had no particular view on the reality of ghosts. He didn't look for them or see them regularly, but with so many souls having been released during the plague years, he was willing to accept they were there. However, he was also pretty sure that spirits didn't look anxious about the effect they had on others, or worry about being seen. Why worry when nothing could touch you any more? When she looked down and saw him squinting up at her, she flinched and looked scared.

She was real. Unlikely and unexpected, but real. It made no difference, as he wasn't going to go chasing after her, and from the look on her face, she was in no rush to meet him either.

It made him uneasy though. Three years ago, when he had left home and come to the city, he had specifically searched out somewhere that was isolated and unpopulated. With so many people gone, you would think that would have been easy, but it wasn't. Many houses had fallen quickly into disrepair, and some people had destroyed their homes rather than let others live there, their final act before leaving.

Once it became clear that the plague had subsided, the survivors had congregated in the same area and concentrated on rebuilding those neighbourhoods, helping one another recreate the human race. Most of the young ones had been taken to the Child Bank. But Max had been raised away from large groups of people, on his family farm. He wanted to see the world beyond it, but that didn't mean full community living.

Was this woman part of a bigger group? Did it mean others were going to come and live here too? It was likely that the population was growing, but he didn't want to start having to share this area with a lot of other people. He hoped this wasn't the start of a new influx. If so, it might be time to consider moving on.

16

As they lay on the narrow bed, Mary could tell that Vander did not actually need her body heat. The shivering was not from cold, and his clammy skin felt cold but hid that he was burning up. His temperature was not dangerously high but was significantly raised. His clothes were damp with sweat, and he was muttering in his feverish half-sleep. She lay across his chest and felt his heart hammering, as if trying to leap through his ribs into hers. She rolled off him, aware that she was elevating his temperature further.

'Don't go.' Vander grabbed her wrist in his hand.

'I'll be straight back. I'm getting you some water. Let me get it. This is something I know about: heartbeats, blood, fever.'

Vander smiled faintly. 'Come back soon.'

Mary made sure he saw her nod, and he released her wrist. Quickly she gathered a bowl of water and the cloth Vander used to wash with. She wet the cloth and wrapped it around his neck above the pulse of blood travelling near the surface of his skin.

She pulled off his clothes, and he neither resisted nor

helped. Reapplying more water to the flannel, she felt his temperature beginning to stabilise. 'Small steps,' she whispered.

Vander pulled her down next to him.

She tried to pull away. 'I'll raise your temperature again. The water will be a waste of time.'

'I don't care. I don't want to be alone.'

She gave in and lay down.

'Vander?'

'Hmm?'

'I know I act like a child ...'

'Hmm.'

'But I'm not. I am grown-up in some ways.'

Vander opened his eyes to look at her. 'Are you taking advantage of my illness?'

'Yes, I think I am.'

She put her hands either side of his face and lowered her face until their noses touched.

'What colour is it?'

'I'm not sure.'

'Let's find out.'

17

Barb pulled the sheet over Scratch and stood and stared at it for a moment. She still expected him to throw it back and shout, 'Surprise! Fooled you!' But of course, he didn't.

She went over to the window and leaned her forehead against the cool glass.

Below, on the grassed area, the young children flocked and spun, fully aware that there was no one to corral them. They leapt and shouted at each other, throwing sticks and keeping busy with the important business of being children.

Over by a tree, a young one sat listlessly leaning against the trunk, and an older sibling came over and felt her forehead.

'So it begins,' Barb said out loud.

From this height, she could see some vans heading up the road towards the Bank. They were white vans with blacked-out windows, and they were travelling fast. Dust and gravel flew out from the tyres as they pulled into the long driveway, barely slowing despite all the children scattering before them. With a bang, the back doors opened, and figures covered in white suits with helmets jumped out of the vehicles.

The children screamed and started running in different directions. Some headed into the building; others ran directly away from it. The figures below split up, following them.

It was as she'd thought. The Facility had a part in this.

She realised that if she stayed, they would either hold her here in quarantine or move her away somewhere and lock her up. Luckily, the scientists did not have a clue how to manage a hundred or so scared children, and at the moment, their attempts to round them up bordered on comedy. There was no coordination or sense of authority. She chuckled as she remembered Scratch being able to stop them all with one word and have them racing to see who could line up and please him first.

The chuckle became a sob.

'Got to go, Scratch.' She walked across and kissed him through the sheet. Then, with a determined air, she headed down the stairs.

Three flights down, she headed along the corridor to the far end of the building and pushed on the fire escape. The heavy door was stiff from lack of use. This floor housed the younger children, and they didn't have the strength to open it, and no one else needed it. Throwing all her body weight forward, Barb finally managed to shift it, and with a few final lunges, there was a gap wide enough for her slim frame to squeeze through.

Behind her she heard muffled shouts as a scientist saw her making her escape, but he was a much larger man in a bulky suit, and he could only wave his arm through the crack. The door was wedged with debris that temporarily jammed it and prevented it opening any further, but Barb decided now was not the time to hang around and find out if his greater force would eventually work.

She ran down the metal steps, skipping over rubbish and jumping the last few to drop to the ground. Her ankle twisted beneath her, but she scrambled up and hobbled towards the trees.

A few of the other children had taken refuge in there too, but she shut her ears to their pleas to stop and headed off into the dense woodland.

Barb was going to find Vander and make him pay for what he'd done, and she needed to be alone to do that. The scientists would eventually round up the children and give them the medicine they needed. They would help them more than she could.

18

We've sealed the Child Bank.

Excellent. How is MARY? I want a full medical to see her status after her little adventure.

We don't have her.

Explain.

She wasn't there.

She escaped again?

No. It seems that she was never there.

But the outbreak. She must have been there, just for a short time.

No. They were all adamant she was never there. A lot of them know Vander Girin-Charris, and they're all certain he

72

never came there with a friend. However, two of the
assistants were very close to him before he moved out, and he
occasionally came back to visit them.

Well then, ask them where he is. He must have confided in
someone.

Unfortunately, one of them, a boy called Scratch, was the
initial case, and he ...

Yes?

Well, he is dead.

Yes, as you say, unfortunate. What about the other one?

The other one is a girl called Barb. She's disappeared.

Disappeared? Before or after all this happened?

After. She came back with this Scratch and looked after him.
It seems that they were partners. When he died, she left.

So she had gone by the time you got there?

Not exactly.

You lost her.

To be fair, we didn't know we needed to keep her.

You were told to seal the Bank.

Yes.

I'm really not sure why I keep you in this job. Fine. Fine.
Well, you had better find where she's gone. And I would do it
quickly. Otherwise, the trail will go cold.

19

U nlike many of the kids in the Child Bank, Barb remembered her life before. She'd been eleven years old when her parents had deposited her.

They had lived in a small house in a wooded area just like this. Her father had been convinced a bad thing was coming for many years before it finally did, and had stocked up in preparation for it. There was a cellar full of dried foods and enough to keep a family going for years. He had been overjoyed when his apocalyptic predictions had come true.

Unfortunately, as time passed and they went on to have more children than planned, the resources ran out much more quickly than expected. Their long-term strategy also failed to be sustainable when it became clear that there had been no thought about how they would live when tin openers became obsolete. A wood was not conducive to growing their own food, and even if they could have cleared some land, they had neither the skill nor the patience to start farming. So when inevitably they began to starve, they had to move to the city to find fresh stores to plunder.

She'd had an older sister, Madge, at one stage, but one night, after much screaming and sobbing, Madge was taken away by her father, and for a time, there was more food again. When Barb asked repeatedly where Madge had gone, her mother finally admitted that Madge had gone to marry the old man in the house at the edge of the woods, where they'd lived originally. Barb knew her sister would never have gone out of choice. He'd been a dirty, smelly specimen who lurked behind trees to leer at them and spat on the ground when they mocked him. Soon after her discovery, Barb went to try to visit her sister but was caught and dragged home. That was the first time she remembered her father taking his belt to her. It wasn't the last though.

When they told her it was her turn to go 'somewhere nice', she feared the worst. So it was quite a relief to find herself at the Child Bank. It was a bit smelly, but there was food and other children, and best of all, she found Scratch.

Scratch made her laugh. He wasn't upset by anything, and he calmed her down. She knew Vander resented her hanging around, but frankly, she didn't care. She wanted to be with Scratch, and she wanted it badly enough to be able to ignore his comments and attempts to push her away. She knew she would eventually win Scratch's affections, so although Vander annoyed her, she understood why he was so angry with her.

Darkness had fallen.

Barb gathered up mulch and leaves, making herself a nest on the ground. It had been a long time since she had needed to do this, but she had slept on the forest floor before, when her parents had been so drunk and angry that it had been a preferable option to staying in the house. She'd been the one who would gather up the younger children and lead them to safety for the night.

She had often wondered what had happened to them after she'd gone to the Bank. She had become especially close to her younger sister, Beal. She could only hope she had made it to another Child Bank or into one of the academies rather than been sold into the arms of a revolting old man.

As Barb dozed, she plotted what she was going to do to make Vander pay for killing Scratch. She wanted to throttle him with her bare hands, but she knew she didn't have the skill or strength to do it.

She needed to be more like a Wucker. It was always fairly obvious which kids at the Bank would be sent to the Wuckenoge Academy. It was the ones with a particularly cruel streak and no qualms about hurting anyone else.

Wucker justice was rough justice. You conformed or you disappeared. There were meant to be prisons somewhere, but no one had seen them or returned to tell anyone what they were like.

She shuddered.

If she couldn't be more like a Wucker, maybe she needed a Wucker to help her. She realised that over the years, she must have known quite a few as they'd passed through the Bank.

There had been one a year or two ago who had followed her around and tried to persuade her to leave Scratch for him. He wouldn't be sorry to hear Scratch was dead, but he might be keen to do her a favour to get into her good books.

It wasn't a great plan, but it was the best she had. The next day, she would go to the Wuckenoge Academy and find him. She'd tell him what Vander had done and ask him to sort it out. It might even get him a promotion if there was a reward for finding them too.

With that decision made, she fell into an uneasy sleep

where Scratch and Vander merged into one and were hunted by the Wuckers.

20

Barb approached the Wuckenoge Academy with extreme trepidation. It had been a long walk through the woods, across the track and up the hilly land looking down over the city. She could have got the train to take her part way, but she didn't want to draw attention to herself too near the Child Bank. She'd stopped at a brook on the way to wash herself down and have a drink. Arriving as a dehydrated, sweaty mess wouldn't serve her plan, and at the moment, it was the only one she had.

The road seemed to go on forever, and she was beginning to think she was lost when she finally came upon the sign. The remaining driveway still seemed to go on forever. Visitors were definitely not encouraged, and even by academy standards, it was a very closed community. Wuckers did not have a reputation for being friendly or sociable. Wuckers liked to be in charge, so unless you liked being pushed around, they were not a group of people you wanted to spend your free time with.

She came to a second gate, this one staffed by a guard who demanded her name and business.

'Barb Girin.'

The guard waited for the second part of her surname. 'Barb Girin what?'

'Just Barb Girin.'

He looked her up and down in a way that made Barb squirm uncomfortably.

'You're a bit old to still be in the Child Bank,' he commented.

Barb wanted to comment that the guard was a bit young to be a Wucker, but she figured goading a kid with a gun was a bad idea.

'Is Shaw here?' she repeated.

'I'll see.'

A message went up to the building, and Barb turned her back and walked a short way from the guard rather than trying to engage in any further conversation.

The last time she had seen Shaw, he had been a scrawny-looking teenager. He was skinny, small and completely unremarkable. The most unusual thing about him had been the idea that he would survive in this place. Shaw turned up much more quickly than she had expected but was pink enough in the face to show he had moved quickly to get there, only slowing for casual nonchalance once in view.

He had changed. He had not only survived but clearly thrived and was now a full head taller than Barb and about twice as wide as he used to be.

'Hello, Barb.'

'Hello, Shaw. I wouldn't have recognised you.' She turned her face to him, knowing her eyes were still red from crying. There was a brief flash of concern, but Wuckers were not meant to show emotion.

He blushed, thrown by her agitation and unsure how to take her comment.

Jerking his head, he indicated that she was to follow him and walk through the checkpoint. Shaw kept his eyes on the guard, and the guard kept his eyes down. *No doubt who was the alpha male between these two*, Barb thought dryly. It was looking more and more like Shaw would be a good person to have on her side, now and in the future. Whatever it took.

At the back of the guard hut, there was another room, which looked like a holding area, with uncomfortable chairs and peeling brown paint. Once out of sight, he put his hand self-consciously on Barb's back to guide her in. She took his other hand, which was missing one digit. All Wuckers had the little finger on their left hand cut off when they were fully trained, to mark them as belonging to Wuckenoge for life. She felt incredibly sad. She ran her fingertips gently over the scar and was sure she felt him shiver.

Shaw turned her to face him. 'What's happened?'

Straight to the point, Barb thought. No messing with the niceties or asking if she was all right.

She had decided to be shameless in appealing to Shaw's attraction to her, but it helped that Shaw was not the spindly kid she remembered. He was all grown up, filled out from good food and exercise, and had a confidence that had grown from his position of power. Barb had a momentary pang of fear that he had outgrown her, but took courage from the fact that he had arrived quickly. More than ever, Shaw wanted to impress, and now it was important to ensure that she seemed vulnerable and in need of protection. She found she didn't have to work too hard on being upset or needing comfort.

As she relived the last few days, the tears flowed, and leaning against Shaw and feeling someone close was consoling. Barb realised that she really did want someone to hold her. He hesitated for a moment, then put his arms around her.

'Vander did something terrible.'

'Really?'

'He killed Scratch.' She pulled back to look at Shaw's face. He nodded grimly. He remembered Vander and Scratch, the golden couple, always scheming together and always resisting his attempts to be part of their group.

She knew she had him hooked.

Scratch was dead.

Vander had killed him.

Shaw could legitimately get rid of Vander.

Scratch and Vander were history.

He struggled to express how he felt about it. 'How ... sad!'

Barb tried to understand the look on his face, but he had learned to hide his emotions well.

'I'm scared Vander will hurt me next. I know where he's hiding, and he doesn't want me to tell anyone. You know how desperate people behave.'

'I can find somewhere safe for you to stay.'

'No. I need to go back to look after the children in the Bank. I work there. But I can tell you where he is, and then you can go and take him in.'

He nodded, but his face was still inscrutable.

'He might start to run if he thinks you know where he is. If you go now, you'll catch him.'

'He won't get far.'

'He's already escaped the Facility security.'

Shaw laughed. 'Well, that's not difficult. They're rubbish. The Wuckers will get him and sort him out. I need to get a team together, but it won't take long.'

'I'm worried the Facility will find him first.'

'Don't be. I told you, they're rubbish.'

'Vander stole something from them. They are desperate to get it back. He said they want to deal with it themselves because they don't want to share it with the other Heads.'

Shaw paused.

'This is big, Shaw. If you can crack it, you'll get the kudos from your boss.'

He loosened his grip a little and thought. 'You wait here. I'll dispatch a squad to deal with it and be back quickly.'

'No.' She put her hand on his chest and ignored his irritation at her contradicting him. 'You don't want anyone else taking credit for this, Shaw. It's big.'

He opened his mouth to point out that he was commanding the squad.

'Plus I want to be certain that Vander will be sorted out. Shaw, you're the only one I trust to do that.' She looked at him with what she hoped was a mixture of pleading and trust.

She threw in her final card. 'I can't relax until I know you've done this for me.'

Shaw reluctantly pulled away, but she could see that the idea of having her beholden to him appealed as much as the revenge and the glory.

She reached up and kissed him. 'I don't want to be alone, Shaw.'

'You don't need to be.' He returned her kiss, holding her tightly so she couldn't pull away or end the embrace. His hands slid down her back, drawing her closer. The buttons of his jacket pressed into her.

'Won't the guard come in?'

'He'd better not,' Shaw growled.

They both knew he wouldn't. Everyone understood that

Wuckers had power and they took the benefits that went with that position.

Barb set her jaw. There was no going back; she had to seal the deal. Shaw watched as she fumbled with the buttons on her top. The blush spread down his neck, turning it into a mass of red blotches, as she dropped it on the chair. The room was freezing cold, and the goosebumps spread over her exposed skin, making her shiver. Shaw removed his jacket and wrapped it around her, enclosing her next to him. On his shoulder, there was a starburst bullet scar.

He followed her gaze. 'Occupational hazard.'

They didn't linger as they came together, both in a rush to beat the cold and embarrassment that threatened to over-take them. Shaw looked dazed at the unexpected turn his day had taken, and Barb just wanted to be consumed with an act that wasn't sickness and death and grief and decay.

When they had finished, Shaw pulled his uniform back on, straightened up and refastened his buttons. 'Where will I find you after we're done?'

Her mind drifted.

'Were you listening?'

She realised Shaw had been speaking, and she shook her head and allowed herself to cry a little more.

More gently he tried again, taking her face in his hand to wipe away the tears and focus her attention. 'I'll sort it out. Go back to the Child Bank. I'll come through in a few days, when I can get some leave. Now tell me where to find him.'

He listened carefully as she explained where the flat was and allowed him to kiss her again and smooth down her clothes before leaving the room. He escorted her back past the guard, who acted as if he had seen nothing. Turning back down the drive, she headed away.

A short way down the road, she heard him shout after her and turned to catch what he was saying. 'Hey, Barb. You did the right thing coming to me.'

She held up her hand in a wave and turned to walk away so he could not see the expression on her face.

21

Wuckenoge has been in touch, and he seems to have found out about our little runaway.

Well, he is in charge of security.

Yes – but I was rather hoping to get MARY back. With his Wuckers on the case, I doubt she will be in one piece by the time they've finished with her. Did you inform him?

No, I did not. I am capable of following basic instructions.

Well, someone did, and he is not too happy to have found it out from this someone.

I did suggest ...

I know you did. On the plus side, the reason he knows about it is that he has been given information about where they are hiding out, and he wants medical backup for his retrieval operation. We need to get a team out to the flats in the derelict district by the river.

Right away.

Do we have that cover story out about the boy?

We do. He is a terrorist who tried to destroy the Facility with a small group of friends from the Child Bank. He escaped and released the germ, and we are working to bring the contagion back under control. The terrorists have been killed, except Vander, who is a wanted man.

Excellent. Well, go and sort out the detail to support the Wuckers. Don't send anyone we can't do without, in case the Wuckers get carried away.

22

Barb didn't go back to the Child Bank but headed to the flats to find a place from where she could watch the arrival of the Wuckers. It was mid-afternoon by the time she arrived.

She decided that hiding within the block might be risky if they did a full sweep of the building. Few safe properties stood in this area beyond the habitable part of the city, but for some reason, this slab of concrete had survived the clearances. There must have been around one hundred flats laid out in a grid, ten up, ten across, with a stairwell at each end. Once it would have had others matching it, but now only rubble and the outlines of walls remained. In the centre of the ruins was an old, overgrown play area. The swings no longer swung and now dangled from one rusted chain, and the roundabout was anchored by the creepers and weeds that had taken hold of it.

In the centre was a climbing frame with an enclosed rope hut at the top. Taking care not to slip on the vegetation, she scaled the ladder and settled down to watch. Looking around the square, she could see all the flats and the four staircases, one in each corner. An archway allowed vehicles in to park around the outer edge, a throwback to the days when ordinary citizens had cars to travel in.

It was wet and uncomfortable, but the damp barely had time to soak into her trousers before the Wuckers arrived.

Her body shook uncontrollably, and she could taste bile in her mouth. She hugged herself and rocked to ease the fear, focusing on the details of the bodies jumping out of the black van. Wearing the uniform black overalls, gloves and helmets, each clutched a rifle, which they held before them as they split up and poured up all four sets of staircases. She had imagined a stealthy approach but could hear the thundering boots pounding the steps even from this distance. It would be amazing if Vander slept through that racket.

Sure enough, after a short delay she saw a third-floor door thrown open towards the end of the level. The two figures came out and headed for the stairs. Straight into their arms, Barb thought with satisfaction. But instead of heading down, she could see them running up two levels and into an empty flat.

As Barb watched, she toyed with the idea of running out to warn the Wuckers, but she quickly ruled that out. By the look of them, they weren't the subtlest team, and they would probably shoot her before realising that she was on their side.

Barb scrambled down from the climbing frame, wiped the green slime from the ropes off her hands and skirted around the edge of the building before making a break for the deserted street. On the other side of the block, she took up a position, curiously watching the flat.

It wasn't long before the window opened and Vander and companion edged out onto the crumbling balcony. They got a bag and swung it out and onto the level below. It was quickly followed by Vander, and after much coaxing, the girl came too.

Vander and the girl were down four levels now and only had the final drop to go. She was surprised and rather impressed. Normally, she would be very happy to see someone get the better of the Wuckers, but it was a bitter irony that the one time she was seeing it was when she had set it up.

Shaw would not be pleased. Worse than that, his bosses would not be pleased. She wondered if he would step up and take the blame alone or decide to share it with her.

It was time to go.

She had walked quite a distance before she realised that she was automatically heading back to the Bank. Home.

Her step faltered, and she looked back to see Vander and the girl heading the other way, towards the river. She could follow them, but her anger was fading and growing numb. She longed to find a sheltered spot and lie down to sleep, succumbing to the exhaustion that was washing over her. Scratch was gone, but the Bank was all she knew, and she needed to go back to her kids and see how they were getting on. Let the Facility and the Wuckers chase them around. For now, she needed to focus on the living and banish the dead from her mind.

23

At first Vander thought the sounds were a trick of his overheated brain. He focused and listened again.

Heavy boots trying unsuccessfully to walk quietly along a concrete walkway.

'Mary, wake up.'

For a moment, she thought she was back in the Facility and the escape was happening all over again.

She tried to block out the urgent whisper in her ear.

'Come on. We have to go.' He shook her.

'No.' She tried to curl up smaller and keep this ball of sleepy warmth close to her. She had been having a lovely dream. She hadn't had many dreams in colour yet; they were still new to her. This one shone with every colour she had ever seen, and for some reason, Vander was blazing red. She instinctively knew that this dream was as fragile as a bubble, and one direct look would make it burst and vanish, along with her chance of ever having one this vivid again. She wanted to stay in her fantasy rather than wake up to reality.

'Mary, they're coming. You have to move *now*.' A hand

grabbed at her clothes and yanked her into her actual life. Cold, hard and about to get worse. The dream was gone instantly.

Automatically she pulled her bag up and moved towards the door, the escape route that they had agreed before she had gone to sleep, with Vander watching fever-ishly over her.

She stumbled after the skinny shadow of Vander as he went out of the door of the flat and made for the steps leading to the other levels, but she bumped into him as he stopped suddenly.

'We can't go down – they're already on the stairs. Up, up.' He let her overtake him and pushed her onwards, nudging her along urgently and quietly.

Her heart was pounding in a way that still frightened her. Another new experience, but less welcome than the dreams.

It was lighter than she had been expecting. Whenever they had talked of moving, it had been planned for night-time. The black. The afternoon sun threw out unexpected shadows that made her flinch, and the dark puddles on the concrete stairs smelt sharp. She didn't know what it smelt of, but she was sure it was nothing nice.

'Where are we going?' She started to panic a little now, and her breath was faster. She didn't like rushing – it made bits of her hurt, and it was confusing. If they were going up, then Vander must think that they could not go down or through the window. This was new territory – they usually had a plan, and so far, it had kept them one step ahead of the scientists.

Vander kept nudging her along, although he didn't need to now. She was wide awake, and her whole body felt as though it was pulsing. She could hear it thumping in time to a more threatening thud of boots coming up from below.

They had reached the fifth floor and Vander pulled her to a stop. Pointing, he indicated that they needed to get down and crawl out of the stairwell and along the walkway.

Mary looked at the filthy floor, strewn with layers of rubbish and dirt. 'Really?'

He nodded, irritation flitting across his face. He jabbed his finger towards the ground again and gave her a small shove. It wasn't a hard push, but it shocked her into movement. Even she could tell that Vander was angry with her now, and despite the more pressing danger, she felt the water spring into her eyes and liquid drip down her nose. Sniffing furiously, she made sure her bag was safely on her back, and then she closed her mind to the nasty things around her and started to crawl along the walkway in front of this level of flats. They moved swiftly, keeping to the back of the balcony to limit the chances of being seen.

Halfway along they came to a derelict flat with a door hanging diagonally off the top hinges. Vander turned his thumb to indicate 'in', and they crawled into the flat, barely stopping to consider that it might already be occupied. They sat up, looked around them and backed up against the wall to sit.

Mary looked to Vander for the next instruction. It never crossed her mind that he might be struggling for an idea. Vander always knew what to do; he always got her out of trouble, and so she waited patiently for his decision. This was Vander's world, and she was still a visitor, learning its strange ways. It wasn't quite what she had imagined it would be, but it was early days, and there had to be better bits than this ... They just had to shake the scientists off, and it would all get easier.

As she waited, she looked around the room. It looked the same as the last one, perhaps a little dirtier, if that was possible. She felt as though she had not seen anything white for a long time.

'Right. They are coming up the stairs at both ends.'

Mary nodded as if she had already thought of that.

'They are going to sweep all the flats to check them, and they will eventually find us ...' Vander faltered. What on earth was he doing? He didn't know how to stay on the run like this. Why was this his responsibility? *Because you made this mess*, he told himself. You knew there would be consequences. He took a deep breath and tried to think of another route. They had bought some time by going up, but there was no avoiding the fact they had to get back down to the ground. On the outside of each flat was a balcony.

'We have to go down these.'

'We're too high up.' She was alarmed to feel the thumping in her body start to speed up again. Why did it do that?

'We go a floor at a time and hope they don't think anyone is stupid enough to go this way.' He waited for her to object, but as usual, she just gave him that trusting look that made him feel sick with responsibility.

'Right, let's go, then.'

'Okay.'

He sighed and went over to the gap where the balcony door had been. The scavengers had even taken the metal from the railing on this balcony, which would make it harder.

'Drop your bag down first.' That was the easy part.

'Who goes first?'

'Me. When I am down, you can drop down, and I'll

catch you.' He didn't even need to look at her to know she accepted that this would work.

He lowered himself as far as he could without looking beyond at the five floors below. His arms ached, and for a crazy moment, he just wanted to let go and put a quick end to all this. If he took Mary down with him, it would all be over.

'Are you all right?' She touched his hand gently.

'Yes.' He swung and dropped over the railing below, landing heavily on the concrete floor.

'Your turn.' He reached up and guided her body down gently until she was safely next to him. For a moment, they hung on to each other, giddy with the success of the plan.

'Only four more to go.'

She thought she saw a small face looking at her through a torn curtain on level two, but before she had a chance to wave, Vander was calling her to drop down.

They continued as silently as they could, grazing elbows and bumping knees until, on reaching the ground, Vander put a finger to Mary's mouth to stop the celebratory shout on her lips.

'We're not there yet.'

She nodded contritely and waited for the next instruction.

He sighed and looked around. 'People are starting to get up for work, so we need to try and find a group and mingle in. No one is looking our way, so they don't know about us.' He paused and looked to check if Mary was listening. He spoke out loud, partly to gather his thoughts but partly to try to help her understand what was going on around her.

'We could go and ask one of them for help.'

'No, we can't.'

'Why not? They look nice.' She looked across at some of

the figures that were moving off up the road towards the station.

'You can't tell what people are really thinking. They could be with the Facility.'

'They are not wearing the Facility suits.'

Vander looked around. It was true that there were no biohazard suits around, so their hunters weren't on to them yet. They needed to get moving before the scientists realised that they had slipped through the net.

'Come on, we need to keep moving. The scientists aren't here, but they may have friends who would tell them where we are.'

'Why would they do that?'

'Because they believe the scientists. They think that they are the good ones.'

'We could tell them the truth.'

Vander laughed. He summed them up from the point of view of a stranger. Two teenagers, both looking grubby and in need of a substantial meal. Vander was tall and skinny, with jeans pulled in tightly to his waist by a fraying belt. He tried to hide this with a baggy T-shirt and jacket. His straight hair stuck out in odd directions except for the parts that hung over his face, partially covering the sharp angles of his almost malnourished features. He felt that he was a fairly average-looking boy, which suited him fine at the moment. Mary, however, was more of a problem. She stood out in so many ways that it was amazing that they managed to hide at all.

Mary was faultless. She had just slept rough and hadn't eaten in hours, but she looked full of energy, her skin practically glowed. *She must be made from Teflon*, he decided. Of course, it didn't help with blending in when she treated each new experience like an overexcited toddler.

She thought that everything was incredible, which made him want to laugh and despair in equal measure.

'Why can't we just tell them the truth?' She was standing beside a lamp post that was flickering on as the day faded. She stood with her face upturned, staring with amazement at the light.

'Because they'd think we were completely mad.' He pulled her away. She spun around and grabbed the only healthy-looking blade of grass from a scrubby patch by the side of the wall. She stroked it and held it up.

Vander glanced around and noticed that she was getting some intrigued looks from the people they were trying to mix with. They had to find somewhere that he could hide her away safely while he got some more food. Perhaps near the riverfront. People just did not group so much any more – safer to keep your distance when you didn't know when the next outbreak might happen. It made it difficult to hide though; bigger crowds would make it easier.

'Please try and walk calmly and just look bored.'

'I can't. It's all too amazing.'

'Stop. I mean it. Do you want to go back to the Facility?'

She looked alarmed. 'No.'

'Then you have to pretend to be bored.'

'Okay.'

She fell into step next to him and took his hand. He could not help grinning to himself – some new experiences were worth getting excited about.

'Is this boring enough for you?'

'Mm.'

'Good.'

He risked a look at her face. She was so beautiful and innocent. Vander felt a pain in his chest. How was he going to protect her? How could he teach her enough to help her survive on her own, because soon she would need to look after herself. He rubbed his chest – the pain was partly emotional but partly physical too.

Mary did not know it, but soon she would be alone.

It wouldn't be today, and probably not tomorrow, but it was certain that by the end of the week, he would be dead.

24

Well?

> *No.*

No?

> *We didn't get them. They were there but they got away.*

The Wuckers didn't get them either. Interesting.

> *It is kind of surprising. I guess someone is going to be in big
> trouble for this one.*

*Well, none of us has much to be proud of at the moment. Do
we know how the Wuckers heard about this or got their lead?*

> *The patrol leader was from your Child Bank. That seems like
> a possible connection, or a coincidence if not.*

Indeed.

Shall I send someone to check it out?

Not yet. I think I might need to make a visit to the Bank. I'll have a think about it. Well, the game is on again. Let's see who is going to get the prize first.

25

Vander sat by the river. They had spent the previous evening walking there and the night catching a little sleep in old archways. Now as the day took hold, the fever did too. It was rising up through him again: lap, lap, lap. Each wave came nearer, threatening to surge over him.

He had left Mary carefully tucked behind some cardboard on the bank. He reckoned he had two hours to find food and more permanent shelter before the water of the river overtook them and made this hiding place useless.

Once again his lack of long-term planning annoyed him. He hadn't really thought this all through when he'd started. He'd just known that he had wanted to get Mary out of the Facility and give her a life, and the moment had presented itself. Luckily, she had no expectations, so he'd succeeded in living up to that low bar. However, in the Facility there was heating, regular nutrition and a bed. He wondered if she wished that she were still there. Perhaps he would ask her. If she wanted to go back, it would solve a lot of problems, including his guilty conscience. At least the sores on her arms had healed now that she no longer had needles stuck in her every day. She had learned to laugh.

Vander got up and started to shuffle along the shoreline, looking down for anything shiny. Last night Mary had nestled up to him, trying to get warm, and they had gone to sleep wrapped around each other. It probably meant very little to her, other than body heat, but for him, it was the closest he could ever remember being to another person. Hugs and kisses had been discouraged after the Red Plague – no intimate contact, even with close family members. He tried to recall being in his mother's arms but couldn't. A vague memory struggled to the surface, of holding his younger brother – before his father had sent him away. He had been a plague orphan. Girls had never given him a second look. Had he sprung Mary from the Facility for cuddles? Of course not ... though was it wrong to hope she might give him the love and affection he wanted so desperately? Just because she didn't know any different, it was still not right to keep her locked away. If only he had planned it better.

He couldn't regret this sense of being really alive for the first time, being able to give pleasure. It was the best feeling ever, and she thought he was good and safe and strong. It was just a shame that he wasn't going to be able to spend long enough with her to break the illusion.

Vander slowed to an amble, out of breath and hardly able to pull each foot from the sucking mud. He had only walked a short distance, but his legs hurt. Perhaps it was time to tell Mary what was happening, so she wouldn't be surprised. He decided to sit down to get the energy for the walk back, but it was more like a collapse, with him dropping onto his bottom and gasping for air. Their time together had been too short. He wanted to be her hero, but he doubted that she even knew what a hero was.

Sitting upright was hard work. Vander lay down, just for a moment. The river mud shifted around his body, moulding into a comfortable, if slightly smelly, bed. If they could get some supplies together, perhaps they should head out of the city. They could find a small place and set up home. If there were no people around, they wouldn't have to answer awkward questions. They could grow things to eat and start their own family, who would love them regardless.

Vander's feet were now so cold that he couldn't feel the water lapping over his shoes and around his ankles. He imagined the sun warming his body as he picked red tomatoes from the plants; he smelt the apples on the trees and listened to the swish of the grass around them. The sound reminded him of the waves of the river as it rose back up the banks. As he fell into unconsciousness, he pictured himself and Mary. She didn't question him or shout at him. She loved him for who he was and for saving her from the Facility. He was all she wanted and all she needed.

As the waves rose, they lifted his body from the riverbed, and quietly he started to float upstream with the incoming tide.

26

We've picked up the body of the boy.

Was he infected?

Yes.

Well, it's what we expected. No sign of MARY?

No. Not yet. But we are focusing along the river. She can't have got far without him.

Hmm. She should have been tagged, and then we wouldn't have this stupid game of hide-and-seek.

We never thought she would be out of the Facility. She wouldn't have been if it hadn't been for the boy. We can only hope that without him to guide her, she will just revert to type and sit and wait till we find her.

May I suggest that we don't sit around hoping and that we damn well get out there and find her?

Of course.

27

Mary was good at sitting. It was, after all, what she had done for about a third of her life.

Lie down and sleep.

Get up and wash.

Sit.

Eat.

Sit.

Eat.

Lie down and sleep.

Repeat.

She would sit and look at the white walls and the white chairs and the white bed. There had been years of practice to get it absolutely right.

Watching the waves of the river gradually move closer was much more interesting than that. They were grey but not one grey, shades of granite and slate and pearl and silver and ash. Vander had given her the words until eventually he had said enough – he would get her a book. He'd had to explain what a book was and had looked really sad that she didn't know what he was talking about. It had felt like a failure on her part, but Vander had said she hadn't been looked after properly. The waves seemed to change colour as they lapped closer, and now that they were only a metre away, she was beginning to get a little anxious. Vander had said that he would be back with some food, and he had never failed to do what he said before.

She didn't know what to do, but it seemed to help Vander when he explained his plans out loud. Perhaps she should try it.

'If Vander is not back by the time the water reaches the smooth stone, I need to move. Otherwise, my feet will get wet.'

She watched closely as the water grew darker and closer. As it touched the stone, she finally began to feel a weight pressing on her chest.

'If I move up onto the walkway, I need to make sure that I can see if Vander returns while staying hidden.'

She edged out of the cardboard and looked around her. She moved towards the steps that led down to the riverfront, and then froze. Ahead of her, against the wall, was a figure.

'If that is Vander, everything will be okay. If it is not ...' Mary became aware of her hands shaking. She looked at them curiously. They had never done that before.

'Are you talking to yourself, or is there someone else in there?'

'Vander should be back.'

'Are you alone?'

Mary had an uneasy feeling that there was a correct answer to this question, but failing to know what it was, she only had the truth.

'Yes.'

'You're talking to yourself. Are you crazy?'

'I don't think so.'

'You're going to get wet unless you get up there soon.'

'Yes.'

'After you.'

Mary went up the stairs. She wished her hands would behave, as the sensation was spreading to her legs and stomach. Close to the top, she stopped to look around as Vander had taught her. She wasn't too sure what she was looking for, but as there were no scientists, she decided it was safe to carry on.

'What now?' The figure had followed up the stairs and was standing behind her. It was a girl, not much bigger than her but much better wrapped up in layers of clothing.

'I don't know. I can't go without Vander.' She looked around as if expecting him to appear.

The girl tilted her head as if trying to measure her up. 'You could shelter in that corner over there for a while. No one will trouble you tonight.' She nodded and walked off.

Mary looked at the corner. It was beneath an overhang and was in shadow. She liked to think that she would have noticed it herself, but she knew she wouldn't have. Turning to thank her mystery helper, she realised she was out of sight.

'If I wait in the corner, I will see when Vander comes back.' She used her foot to shift the debris and check for anything nasty. It was mostly old newspaper, and so she backed into the gap and waited. Vander would be really impressed that she'd found a spot like this. Perhaps she didn't need to tell him that it hadn't been her idea.

It was really getting dark now. She looked up into the blackness above. The sky had been switched off for the night. Every time she looked up there was a new surprise, another shape or colour emerging from the vast space. She wished she had more words to describe it.

She looked up as she heard a motorboat moving slowly

down the river. It had a searchlight that was sweeping the banks, backwards and forwards. Instinctively she shrank back against the wall and made herself as small as she could.

As the night closed in, she dozed, woken occasionally by sounds on the river.

'NO SIGN OF YOUR MATE, THEN?'

It was light and cold. Mary shifted, and it forced a hard, deep noise out of her mouth that seemed to fit the feeling in her arms and legs. She had meant to stay awake and watch, but it was hard to make her eyes stay open after the sun had gone away. She looked around, sure that Vander would be nearby.

'He should be here.'

'Looks like he's abandoned you.'

'He wouldn't do that. He wouldn't.'

'Then something's happened to him.'

'The scientists must have him.'

The girl raised her eyebrows, and Mary wished that she could snatch the sentence back. She wasn't meant to talk about the scientists – this might be one of their friends.

The girl turned to walk away.

'Wait. What do I do?'

The girl frowned. 'It's not up to me.' She turned again.

'Please.'

'Look, you must have friends somewhere.'

'No.'

A smaller person appeared next to the girl. 'She could come with us, Beal.'

'No, she couldn't.'

'Please.'

She gave Mary a hard look. 'You don't even know me.'

Mary's look was open and trusting. 'I do. You're Beal.'

Beal gnashed her teeth and said something to the smaller person that made her flinch and move away from her. 'We don't need another mouth to feed.'

'She's pretty; people might give her things. Not like you – you're too ugly.' This time, the small one jumped away quickly before the punch landed on her.

'You look after her, then. I can't be explaining everything twice to two morons.'

'All right, Beal, we know you are the one with the clever brain. That's why God made you so ugly, to balance it out.'

'Give me strength.' Beal rolled her eyes and marched away.

The small girl took Mary's hand. 'Come on. My name's Cress.'

Mary allowed herself to be pulled along. 'What is God, Cress?'

'God looks after us all.'

'He's not doing a very good job of it,' Beal shouted back.

'He does it secretly,' Cress said defiantly.

'The scientists used to look after me.' The thought set Mary's stomach growling, and she stopped in alarm. 'My middle's talking.'

'I wish the rest of you would shut up,' Beal snapped.

'Let's try her out,' Cress shouted back.

'Okay, your project. Off you go.' Beal leaned against a wall and folded her arms.

'Right. You need to go up to someone and say that you've lost your bag and please could you borrow the money for a bus?'

'But I haven't lost my bag.'

'Well, obviously.'

'So why am I saying that?'

110

'Because it's rude to just ask for money. It's begging.'

'So it's rude to just ask for money, but it's okay to lie.'

'Yeah, you've got it.'

Beal shifted her slouch. 'You don't need to get it; you just need to do it.'

'Oh, okay.' Mary started to walk away.

'Hang on. We need to pick who you're going to ask.'

'Who do you think?'

'That man. He's young and smart, and he might fancy you enough to do it.'

'What?'

'Trust me. He's the one. Go on. Do it.'

Mary started towards the man. Cress was right – he looked nice. She glanced back, and Cress nodded and smiled. About ten paces from him, a girl stepped in front of her and took his hand. Mary faltered. She glanced back towards Cress, who was now waving her arms around, which Mary guessed meant to carry on.

'Hello.' The couple turned to look at her. The man looked quizzical, but the woman looked cross.

'Well?' The woman broke the silence.

'Um. I've lost my bag. Please could you give me some money for a bus?'

'Give?'

Mary froze. Cress hadn't said 'give'. 'I meant borrow. Please could I borrow some money?'

'No, I think you said what you meant the first time,' the woman said coldly.

Mary started to back away under the ferocity of the woman's glare.

'Look, here.' The man held out some paper.

'Fergus. She's begging.'

'No, I'm not begging; I'm lying.' The man laughed,

which seemed to make the woman even angrier. Mary could tell that this wasn't going well.

'Just take it. Come on, let's get going.'

He thrust the paper into Mary's hand, and they turned with one final glower from the woman.

Mary hurried back over to Cress, who had her hands pressed hard against her eyes.

'Is it all over?'

'I'm back.'

Cress removed her hands. 'Oh, you weren't arrested. That went well.'

'Did it? I thought it was going wrong.'

'It did go wrong.'

'Oh. But you just said it went well.'

'That was sarcasm.'

Mary's head hurt. She didn't like this game very much. 'He gave me this.' She held out the paper. 'Is it rubbish?'

Both Beal and Cress stared. 'That's twenty pounds.'

'Is that good?'

Cress sighed. 'You need a lot of lessons. Yes, it is very good. Against all odds, you hit the jackpot. Come on, let's get some food to stop your middle talking.'

28

The latest case is Fergus Wiltshaw. He is critical but so far still alive. It seems she approached him for some money, and he gave her some. That was not far from the river. It's possible that the boy's body was carried upstream from around here the night before. His contacts have been quarantined and are being monitored. He gave her twenty pounds, which is obviously very inconvenient, as she could have travelled quite a distance with that sort of sum. We are monitoring CCTV at the stations to establish whether she got a train, and if so, in what direction.

In other words, she could be anywhere.

Yes.

29

Less than half a kilometre from the river, and not far from the flat she had escaped from, Mary sat in a hall that had been divided into cubbyholes and various spaces by sheets and assorted furniture.

'Welcome to the community hall. It hasn't been used as a hall since we last had a community.' Beal pointed to an area under the window. 'That bit's free. Cress will help you get sorted.'

'Who's that?' a hostile voice shouted from under a pile of blankets. 'We're full. Don't go letting any more in.'

'This, everyone, is Mary. She contributed our food this evening, which is more than you did, Ned, so back off.'

Mary looked around to see a few faces peering out.

Suddenly the door banged open. 'They found a floater.' A boy came racing into the room. 'They pulled it out, but get this: they all had big suits on, you know, not *suit* suits, with ties, but big white suits, covered all over, with helmets and everything.' He gasped for breath and saw Mary. 'Who are you?'

Beal stepped between him and Mary. 'This is Mary, Fix, and you need to stop talking.'

'But it was weird, really spooky, like a horror film.'

'STOP NOW!'

Fix looked hurt for a second, then shrugged. 'Great, food.' He moved to the table and started eating without a second look.

Beal turned to Mary.

'What's a floater?' Mary asked.

'A dead body,' one of the smaller children shouted out with glee. 'What did it look like, Fix? Was it all green?'

There were squeals and shouts from the other children as they crowded around to hear the answer. Fix looked around at his captivated audience and purposefully sat down, ready to tell his tale. He pulled his coat off slowly and pushed it beneath him, where no one could steal it.

'Come on, Fix, tell us what you saw.' They leaned in to hear.

'It was hard to see. They were trying to keep us all back, away from it.'

Some children started to move away, suspecting there was nothing to this story.

'But I sneaked in under the cordon.' He reeled them back in. 'He wasn't green.'

'You could see it was a man?'

'Better than that. I know who it was.'

The silence stretched as they waited for the reveal.

'It was Vander.' To a few of the older children who had run away from the Child Bank, this was big news, and they started to explain to the others that he was one of their own, an alone child, the orphaned or abandoned, the escapees from abuse in broken families or the Bank itself.

Mary felt a hand grip her arm painfully and pull her backwards, but she resisted, wanting to catch what Fix was saying. It didn't make sense. She wanted to hear more.

Some of them had seen the posters and, more remarkably, had been able to read them. 'What, that terrorist from the Child Bank?'

'Vander wasn't a terrorist.' Fix looked grim.

Others began to realise where they'd heard the name mentioned on the streets and in the stations where they found their scraps. 'He was. He tried to blow up the Facility and let all the germs out. I heard it.'

A girl pushed forward. 'I knew Vander too. He was nice. He didn't hurt people.'

'Ah, what do you know? You ever been to the Child Bank?'

'Yes, I have.' She stuck out her chin. 'I was there, but they were just growing us to make us do their work. Everyone said.'

No one disagreed with her. The Child Bank had a bad reputation for having a lot of children who disappeared.

'They gave us food every day. Why would I leave that if it was so good?'

There was some muttering, but they all knew nobody left a free meal unless the risk outweighed the full stomach.

'Vander was one of the good ones,' she continued. 'Him and his friend Scratch were good.'

'I heard everyone at the Child Bank got sick,' another voice chimed in. 'No one will go up there at the moment, and no one's seen any of the kids come out.'

This news sent a shiver around the room.

'It all comes from the Facility. That place is bad.'

As Mary tried to open her mouth, Beal yanked her hard towards the back of the hall. She drew a curtain aside, revealing a large space with a lumpy mattress and piles of cushions, which she pushed Mary down onto.

Beal closed her eyes for a second, took a breath and then looked at Mary, who was trying to get up again.

'Stay put. We need to talk.'

The wall behind them was covered in bright sheets and scarves. Mary reached out her hand and stroked them. 'What is this?'

'What do you mean? It's just material.'

'What colour?'

Beal shook her head. 'Purple. It's purple. Mary, where have you been that you don't know about colours, or money, or basic stuff about how to live?'

Mary wondered whether it was sensible to tell her secret. For a moment, she tried to think of an alternative answer, but there was nothing. What could she say instead?

'I lived in the Facility with the scientists.'

'Worked there?'

'No. Lived there. Always lived there. It was my home, I suppose. Vander started to work there, but he got me out because I'd never seen the sky. He said it wasn't right.'

'But what about your parents? Were they there too?'

'I don't think I have parents.'

'Is the Facility a prison?'

Mary shook her head, confused.

'Had you done something wrong? Something bad?'

Mary thought for a minute. 'I don't think so. I never did anything; I just sat. What did Fix mean about Vander? Is he coming here soon?'

'It might not have been Vander. Fix might not have seen the body properly.'

Mary shook her head. 'Body?'

Beal gazed up at the ceiling, weighing up her words. 'Vander is probably dead, Mary. Do you know what that means?'

Mary shook her head.

For a moment, they sat. Beal pinched the bridge of her nose, then looked up at Mary. 'It means his body has stopped working. He's gone and can't help you. I'm sorry, Mary, but he can't help you any more.'

Mary felt a new sensation in her stomach, a clenching tightness that gripped her middle and made her bend over. 'The scientists got him. We were running away from them. They want to take me back to the Facility, and Vander said we had to stay away. They're chasing us and want to catch us.'

'Do you think they killed him?'

Mary shook her head, more in confusion than as an answer.

They sat for a few minutes. Water splashed from Mary's eyes. 'Why are my eyes leaking?'

'They're tears. It's what happens when we're sad. You miss Vander, so you're upset.'

'I don't like this feeling. I don't like my middle talking or having to ask new people for money. It's all strange outside the Facility, but not all of it's very nice. Perhaps I should go back.'

Beal looked at her for a few moments.

'Life is a big, mixed-up bag. Some of it is bad, but there are the good bits that come along and make you forget that, at least for a while. If you hadn't left, you wouldn't have had time with Vander at all.'

'Vander used to bring me my food, but he wasn't meant to talk to me, really. He did though, just a bit, and some-times he held my hand.'

'Whatever they were doing with you in that place, they weren't giving you a good life. Vander was right. You should be allowed to do things.'

'Is this a good life?'

Beal laughed. 'It could be better, I guess. It would be nice to have more money, food, stuff like that.'

'But people give you money.'

'They give *you* money. Cress was right – they take one look at me and run away.' She laughed. 'Could you choose if you stayed in this Facility or went somewhere else?'

'No. I didn't even know that there was somewhere else. I thought everyone lived in a facility. Vander told me it could be different. He told me that things changed.'

'He was right. You can change things if you want to, or at least you can try to. You've made it this far, Mary. Don't just give up now.'

Her stomach rumbled loudly.

A shout came from the hall. 'Hey, food's here. Come on, Mary, get here and share it out before this lot steal it.'

'Go on with you. Go and get the glory. This one is on you.'

Mary got up and pulled the sheet back to go across the hall again. As she came out, a man brushed past her as he went in. He smelt strongly of dirt and other new odours, but nevertheless, Beal put her arms around his neck and kissed him.

He looked back and watched Mary leave. 'New recruit? You been busy?'

'You have no idea. I'll tell you later.' The sheet fell back, hiding them from sight.

Mary went across to the table where steaming paper parcels sat. She wiped the last of the tears away with her palms.

'Here. We've got fish. Give each of them some, like this.' Cress pulled a piece off and dropped it into an outstretched hand. 'Where's your manners?' she lashed out.

'Thank you,' the small child shouted back as he ducked her swing.

'You do it. You got the money for it.'

Mary stepped up and tried to break a bit off but withdrew her hand sharply. 'Ow. It hurts.' She put the sore fingers in her mouth.

'It's just hot. Do it quickly from the edges. Come on, we're all starving.'

'Do it. Do it.' The mass of children jostled one another, holding out grubby hands to receive their share.

Mary started breaking off bits of fish for the children, guided by Cress, who stopped her giving out too much at once and sent the chancers coming for seconds to the back until they'd all had some. Cress sent a small messenger behind the curtain with some of the food.

Mary worked out that licking her fingers between each serving stemmed the heat, and no one complained until the last boy in line.

'I don't want your lick,' he grumbled. 'I'll break off my own.'

'We'll be watching, Ned. Mind you only take the same as everyone else,' Cress warned. He made a big show of measuring out a piece and breaking it, but Mary saw he managed to slip a little extra under his hand and walked away with twice as much as anyone else.

Finally, there was only Mary and Cress left. 'Split the rest in two,' she instructed Mary. Leaning across, she took the larger piece. 'The manager always gets the biggest share.' She laughed. 'Eat up, or they'll swipe it from under your nose.'

Mary ate the remainder with her fingers. She barely had enough energy to swallow, and having finished, she just wanted to curl up on the spot and sleep.

Cress had arranged a pile of blankets in a crumpled heap, which Mary buried down into until she couldn't see anyone or anything. She never wanted to come out again. She ached. Her eyes ached and her insides ached. That night, she found out what it was like to fall asleep crying.

A vivid dream overwhelmed her. In it she floated slowly upwards, flying above the city. Down below her she could see the river gently moving backwards and forwards, in and out as if it were a living, breathing thing. She could see the community hall, holding lots of little figures, and the train track that they'd walked along after getting the money. Cress had said that if you followed it all the way down across the bridge over the river, you came to a reservoir, where the city's water came from. Mary wanted to follow it now, but out of the corner of her eye, up the opposite end of the tracks, she could see a white building tucked between the trees on the hill above the city.

She tried to turn away, but it dragged her back, pulling her towards it. Gradually she was floating in its direction as if being sucked in. She swam in the air, kicking and flailing, but still it got nearer. Suddenly the drag became stronger and faster, and she started to panic as she realised that she had no control over where she was going. She could see the exit they had run through, the corridor, the sliding doors, the locks and computer pads, and finally her room, which she had walked away from only a few days ago. In that room was a bed with straps for her legs and arms, and now she was trapped, tied down and unable to move any more.

She could hear someone approaching. Their footsteps were soft in the fabric shoes, but their legs swished as they rubbed together, because of the bulk of the suit. A scientist. They turned in through the doorway, holding a huge tray of needles before them, which they put on a table by the bed.

121

She couldn't see the face through the mask, but there was a sound like laughing coming from under the hood.

He started to tap and stroke her arms and legs, looking for a vein to stick the needle into. She started to struggle, but he held her tighter, squeezing her. 'Stop struggling. Keep quiet.'

She started to buck, twisting her body, and suddenly she was awake and realised that the hands and voice were real. Someone had pulled back the blanket layers of her cocoon, gradually peeling them away.

She tried to wriggle down into the mound, but a hand reached in and clamped over her mouth. 'Don't make a noise, and I won't hurt you. I just want to see what we've got here. Shout, and you'll be sorry.'

30

Mary lay still, muscles tensed but unmoving as the man ran his hands over her body. She wanted to cry out but was too scared. Around her, there was almost no sound, just the occasional mutter and rustle as children shifted into more comfortable positions. She could feel a cold draught now the covers had been pulled back. There was a damp smell in the air, and the waft of rancid sweat from the man, who was pushing his face close to hers.

'You're a bit shinier than the usual ragbag we get around here.'

Mary's eyes were adjusting, and she could make out some of his features. It looked like Beal's friend who she'd passed earlier.

'Ah, you do recognise me. Well, we can get this clear, then. Beal doesn't need to know about this. Just a chance for us to get to know one another a little better.'

He lay on top of her, squashing the air from her lungs. 'If I take my hand away, you're not to make a sound. Understand?'

She nodded.

He took his other hand, and grasping her little finger, he twisted it back and around, bringing tears to her eyes. 'This is a taster. You make a noise, and I will really hurt you. Nod if you'll be quiet.'

She nodded again and rubbed her finger. She had almost forgotten real pain, and it brought a painful vision of a white room and needles.

'Good.' Hesitantly he removed his hand from her mouth, and she gasped for breath. 'Looks as if it's my lucky day. A hot meal and a hot girl.' He chuckled at his own wit.

Mary thought back to all the times in the Facility when she'd been trapped while men in suits did unpleasant things to her, taking samples or expecting her to stand still in cold rooms or lie on hard benches while they prodded, poked or just stared at her naked body. Then she remembered that in the Facility, she had perfected the art of pulling her mind away and pretending that she wasn't in that body being violated. She could lie or sit nearby, separate and unaffected. So she took herself back to those moments, and now it wasn't her that was being rubbed and stroked by this man, until in frustration he slapped her hard across her face, and she was back.

He pressed his mouth up close to her ear. 'I don't mind if you join in or struggle, long as you're quiet about it. I can't stand this pretending you're a plank of wood.' He grabbed her hair and pulled it back. 'Do you understand?'

She nodded.

He kept his hands in her hair and brought her face up to his. She tried to stop taking in air, as his breath stank. He rubbed his face against hers, and she grimaced as the patchy stubble sanded her skin. Despite herself, she let out a whimper.

'That's better.' He grinned.

He pressed his mouth to hers, and she closed her eyes and mouth as tight as she could, and he came away leaving spit on her lips. She took a breath, and he seized the moment to push his mouth to hers again while it was open, pushing his tongue into it. Without thinking, she bit it. Hard.

Screaming, he jumped up holding his mouth. He leapt about, swearing and kicking her with big, heavy boots. She curled up with her hands over her head to protect her face until, wrenched upright, she had to look at him again.

'You're going to be so sorry you did that.' Each word was an effort, and there was a dribble of blood and saliva running down his chin. 'Beal told me about you. You won't last two minutes out there on your own. Or maybe we should get in touch with these scientists. Perhaps there's a reward for you.'

Silently and urgently she shook her head.

'Too late. You should have thought about consequences before, shouldn't you?'

He threw her down on the blankets, and her head hit something hard. She lay dazed on the ground.

'What's going on?' Beal stood nearby. Mary looked up and felt relief that once again Beal was going to help her.

'What's up, Pen?'

'Nothing. Couldn't sleep. Thought I'd check our new visitor was all right. Seems she's feeling a bit homesick. She'll be leaving in the morning.'

Mary turned to Beal in confusion, but the look she got back was closed and showed no emotion. Around them a few sleepy heads had lifted above their nests to see what the fuss was about. 'No. I can help you get money. You need me.'

Beal spoke to the space above her head. 'We were

getting along fine before you came along. It seems you bring a lot of trouble with you. Get some sleep. You need to find your own place tomorrow.' She turned to the faces around them, shouting, 'That goes for all of you. Get your heads down, and mind your own business unless you want to go too.'

She turned around and stormed back to her corner. Pen gave her a satisfied smirk and followed her.

Mary lay, dizzy with confusion. She realised that she could taste Pen's blood in her mouth, and she rolled towards the floor and spat again and again to try to rid herself of it.

She was too tired to fight sleep and lay on top of her bedding, drifting in and out of wakefulness. A couple of times, she thought she heard the sound of a helicopter hovering above them before moving off again.

Finally, she woke. The sun was up, but there was no sound or movement around her. It was quieter than it had been all night. It was too quiet. Something was wrong. She sat up quickly.

Looking around, she could see that everyone still seemed to be in the hall. There was a hand or foot sticking out from beds around her, and she could see the tops of some of their heads. She stood and looked around. No mumbles, no tossing, no turning. Nothing and no one stirred.

'Hello?'

Nothing.

Shakily she walked across to Beal's corner. Pen's booted foot was sticking out from under the sheet. Thinking about the previous night, she tapped it. When nothing happened, she gave it a harder kick. It felt hard and unyielding, like a stone.

'Beal?'

Still nothing.

Gathering her courage, she took the edge of the sheet and quickly pulled it back. Pen lay on his back, his eyes wide, his mouth open as if trying to catch as much air as possible. He was dead. She poked him hard to make sure, but he was stiff and cold. Next to him lay Beal. Mary fought the sick feeling inside her and slowly reached out to touch her.

Beal was clammy but still soft and living. Mary shook her gently but got no response. Beal's breaths came irregularly and sharply. Each one was an effort, and the gaps between them were painfully long.

Mary backed away and slowly turned to look around the room. She suspected that the bodies were a mixture of those who were already dead, and those who teetered on the line between life and death, and could still fall either way. Her own breathing had speeded up, and the oxygen was making her light-headed.

Pen had reckoned that she couldn't survive without them. Well, now she would have to. She knew she could get money if she needed to, but with a flash of clarity, she realised there might already be some here.

Going back over to Beal's area, she saw a box on the floor behind her. She braced herself and leaned across to open it. Sure enough, there was paper and coins inside. She took it all and went back to find her bag. After grabbing a thin blanket and rolling it up, she pushed that in too. Finally, she spotted a woollen hat on the table. Everyone had commented on her hair. Maybe it was time to become less obvious. She pulled it down over her head. She grabbed a packet of biscuits, and without a further look, she left.

31

Max had watched the girl across the road for the past ten minutes. Twice she'd got up and walked towards the old community centre before turning around again and returning to her spot on the wall.

At one point, she talked to herself for a while and then stamped her foot in anger before sitting down and crying.

He was fairly sure it was the girl that he'd seen at the window in the flats. He could see her more clearly at this distance. She still had incredibly pale skin that looked almost translucent – no wonder he had thought she was a ghost.

Max hadn't expected to see her again after the raid the other day. He'd returned to find his flat ransacked and most of his possessions broken. They'd held and questioned him for several hours, and the only good thing was missing the actual assault, as doubtless he would have been shot. They'd been after someone called Vander, and Max never wanted to hear that name again. By the time they'd established his real identity and whole life history, he'd lost a night's sleep and had a miserable day at work the next day, trying to stay awake.

He couldn't watch any longer. It was too painful to see someone who was obviously so upset, but he had to leave for work soon. He had five minutes – time to see if there was anything he could do.

'Are you all right?'

She looked up, taking a moment to focus. She held her hand up and turned her face away. 'Don't come any nearer.'

'I won't hurt you.'

She turned to face him. 'No. I might hurt you.'

He laughed nervously. She was obviously mad. 'Do you need help?'

'I have to go, but something terrible has happened in the hall.' She looked back at the community centre.

'What? What's happened?'

'I don't know, but they need help.' She seemed relieved to have said it.

'I've got to go. Tell them to get the Facility here.' She turned and started to run down the road away from the centre.

'Wait. What facility?' But she was gone.

He looked at his watch. Four minutes. Did he have time? Not really, but what if something had happened? He started to walk towards the community centre and got as far as reaching for the wonky handle. A cold feeling washed over him. For a moment, he stared at the peeling paint on the door, and at that moment, he decided that he was the most cowardly man he knew. He sighed and turned back to walk to a communal phone at the corner, where he could call the Wuckers. Now he was going to be late for work because a madwoman was running around outside his house, claiming something was wrong in that crazy community centre, which always had something going on in it anyway. He paused. Perhaps it was nothing. He dialled.

'Hi. It may be nothing, but I think something's going on in the hall down by the river.'

Twenty minutes later he was on his way to work and glad to get away from the chaos that had broken out down the road. There were helicopters, ambulances, and people in suits and masks sealing off the centre and the ground around it. He hadn't given his name or revealed that it was him who had called, as he had no intention of coming to their attention again. He suspected that they'd think it was too much of a coincidence to be caught up in this mess twice. His conscience twinged as he wondered if he should have told them about the girl. Perhaps she had hurt those kids. Somehow he didn't think so. Otherwise, she wouldn't have stuck around but would have just run away and not wandered about outside.

Luckily, the sirens and helicopters backed up his story to his supervisor, and he was soon behind the counter in the ticket office.

'I need to get to the reservoir.'

He looked up to see the crazy girl. He glanced around, expecting to see police running in behind her. 'You.'

'Thank you for getting the help.'

'Are you in trouble?'

'I didn't do anything.'

'Then why didn't you call the Wuckers?'

'I didn't know how.' She looked tired, and there was a blossoming bruise on her cheek. 'I guess I am in trouble. I just want to go somewhere quiet, away from all this noise.'

'The reservoir is near Lakeside station, last on the line. It's five pounds. Do you have the money?'

'She held out some coins. Is this enough?'

'Yes. Push it through.'

'No. I don't want to give it to you.'

'No one ever does. You have to give me the money, or I can't give you the ticket.'

'But this money is dirty.'

He shook his head. 'I touch money all the time.'

'I don't want it to hurt you. You've been kind to me.'

He looked at the lengthening queue forming behind her. 'The only other way is to do it through the machine. Say where you want to go, and put the money in.'

She looked back where he was pointing. 'Lakeside?'

'Lakeside.'

He watched her briefly as she walked across to the machine, and then she was lost from sight as passengers milled around the concourse.

32

She could have gone miles, but in fact, she was just a few hundred metres from where the boy's body must have entered the river.

Yes.

How did we miss that?

We had no way of knowing where she had gone.

But she was alone and had no idea how to get around.

Well, yes.

And in the meantime, what is the current damage?

We have thirteen fatalities and three in isolation.

Are they likely to recover?

Could go either way.

So far, in fact, we have isolated cases except for a bunch of kids that nobody cares about. You could argue that we have caused a substantial drop in the cases of street theft and begging. However, someone will notice a problem pretty soon unless we get this situation under control now. Do we have any idea where she could be?

She was caught on camera buying a train ticket at the station.

Where to?

Lakeside.

Well, better follow the breadcrumbs, then.

Breadcrumbs?

Never mind. Find out if she got there.

Right.

Marinda turned away from her keyboard, took a deep breath and massaged her temples in an attempt to relieve the stress headache that had been threatening to kick in all day. Communications with her deputy always set them off.

How had she ended up with such incompetent staff?

Three obvious reasons, she answered herself.

Firstly, there really just were not that many people to choose from any more. The Red Plague had taken a lot of the adults, and it hadn't been discerning about its victims.

Rich, poor, clever, stupid: it made no difference. If it got you, it got you.

Secondly, she didn't have much money to spend on security. The money went into the science labs, and even they were run on a shoestring. The Child Bank did little more than break even. It cost a lot to look after all those kids, and farmers and small-scale factories didn't pay much for the labour when they bought kids. She wondered for the millionth time whether it was worth carrying on with them, but she felt, on balance, it was. It gave her a sort of loose control over a lot of kids, both financially and in terms of what they learned.

Thirdly, and finally, having someone too bright as her assistant might create its own problems. She had no intention of handing her little empire over to anyone else after all the work of setting it up. She had no doubt it could be done better, so anyone too sparky or ambitious was a threat. Better to lord it over the weaker mortals than watch out for a stab in the back.

Nevertheless, at times like this, it would be really nice to think her staff would find the girl and get everything back under control. As she knew they wouldn't, she was just going to have to get out there and do it herself.

Back out among the great unwashed, she told herself, and shuddered. *Time to try out that new vaccination.*

33

Mary pulled the hat down further over her hair and followed the other passengers. They walked through, stopped and stood still. She used to be good at standing still, but suddenly this seemed to be the hardest thing she had ever done. Mary glanced at those around her, trying hard not to move her head. It felt like every time she looked at someone, they turned away quickly. She tried to catch a couple out by moving suddenly, but that just made more people peer at her curiously. She was on the verge of running when, with a rush, a huge metal container thundered towards them and came to a stop with a screech.

She allowed herself to be pushed onto the train, then scuttled to the far end of the carriage, trying to distance herself from as many passengers as possible. Curling up upon herself, she bent her head down and tried to make herself invisible. Gradually she became aware that a small person had sat down opposite and was leaning towards her.

'What did you do?' he snarled. 'You knew the floater.'

Then she remembered him. 'You're Ned.'

'They were my friends. Beal looked after us. She looked after you. She let you stay.'

'She was going to make me go away.'

'So you hurt her.'

Mary became aware that Ned's voice was getting louder. His fists were clenched, and his face was becoming redder as tears started to run down his cheeks.

'No. I didn't. Please don't get angry. I didn't hurt them.'

'They were fine. They were all fine.' The sound of the train had been covering their talk, but now, as it pulled into a station, the background noise fell. 'And then you come, and they're all … they're all … *dead*.'

Mary saw that some of the other passengers had heard Ned's words.

'Please, Ned.'

'Please what?'

'Please stop. People are looking.'

'You kill my friends, and you want me to be nice to you.' Ned was standing in front of her, swaying as the train moved off again.

'I didn't do anything.'

'You're bad. Why are you alone? Why did your friend end up floating in the river? Why is everyone around you dead?'

She shook her head. 'I don't know. I don't. I really don't.'

'You're bad.' Ned wobbled and staggered. Mary held out her hand to steady him, but he hit her away. Ned sat heavily down on the seat opposite. He was no longer red but a shade of grey that Mary wasn't sure that she could describe. His curly hair was wet with sweat, and all the fight had gone out of him.

'Ned, I think you need to go to the Facility.'

'The place you escaped from? No, thanks.'

'I don't know why ... but I think you're right. The people around me get sick.'

'It's you.'

'Maybe you're right.'

Ned leaned against the glass, and a halo of steam formed around his feverish head. He talked with his eyes closed. 'Did the people at the Facility get sick around you?'

'I didn't see it ... but ...'

'But what?'

'The usual people had suits on, and the one's that didn't ... they didn't stay long.'

'What about your friend?'

'He didn't wear a suit.'

'They died.'

Mary looked out of the window. The idea that all the real people she'd met were dead was too painful to discuss, think about or process. No one had been as special as Vander, but Ned was right – they had helped her, and now they were gone. Was it her fault?

It was now that she truly realised that it had only been Vander who'd seen her as a person. She turned back to Ned. His eyes were closed, and he was slumped in the corner.

'Ned?'

He didn't move. The train was pulling up again, and there were very few people left in the carriage.

'Last stop, Lakeside.'

Mary picked up her bag and moved towards the exit. On the platform, she saw a man in uniform.

'Do you work here?'

'Yes.'

'There's a boy in that carriage who isn't very well.'

The man turned, and Mary walked towards the exit. It was so quiet. As she left the station, she looked around and wished that Vander were here so she could ask him for more words to describe the colours that bombarded her eyes.

34

We found another contact on a train.

Alive?

Not by the time we secured the site. Unfortunately, he'd been touched by the staff at the station, and obviously, there are likely to have been a large number of contacts travelling in the carriage.

Can we trace them?

Not really. It will be a waiting game to find victims as they fall, so to speak.

Unfortunate.

Well, yes, I'd consider it pretty unfortunate if I were a passenger, or their work colleague or a member of their family.

Then I suggest you find her and stop her.

We are close.

Not close enough. The only thing to be salvaged from this is
data on the effects of releasing MARY into the population. I
assume we are logging the results systematically.

Of course. Although ...

Yes?

Another week of data would be more meaningful. I mean—

I understand what you mean.

We might not get this sort of opportunity again.

There is no intention of that, certainly. All right. Find
MARY urgently, but once we have her under surveillance,
she can be observed for one more week. In the meantime, if it
looks like the situation might escalate, she can be brought in
sooner.

Excellent. Thank you.

You still have to find her.

Yes.

So do it.

35

As Barb approached the Child Bank, the silence was painful. Not a shout, nor a scream. No laughter. No calling out. No noise.

She almost turned and ran. Then she thought about Scratch and how he would never leave the little guys at a time like this. Pushing forward, she went into the building.

The smell was almost too much to bear, so she slipped into a store cupboard to find cotton to breathe through. The shelves had been ransacked, although most of the stock was still there but on the floor, not the shelves. She saw a thick cotton pad, which she pulled out of the confusion and slipped into a surgical mask, which she put over her mouth and nose.

Back out in the corridor, she moved slowly along, bracing herself for a scene of horror around each corner. Occasionally she found a small body curled up. She checked each for life and, finding none, put a cloth over their face.

Every one of them looked like they had fallen asleep after getting a little too flushed and excited.

On the next floor, she found another six bodies. Her

heart rate was rising. Where were all the other children? Was she still going to find them further up? Had they all run away?

As she turned the next corner, she heard a whimper. Curled in the turn of the stairs was one of the younger children.

'Hey.' She leaned towards her to hug her and check if she was all right, but she shrank from her with a look of terror on her face.

'Don't come near me,' she cried out. 'You was with Scratch before he died. You've got the sickness.'

Barb sat back. She could be right, but so far, she felt okay. From start to finish, Scratch had taken sick and died very quickly. She racked her brain to think if she knew how fast the Red Plague was meant to take you, but it was so long ago now, and no one had really wanted to talk or reminisce about it.

This fear was going to get them nowhere though. 'If you are going to get it, it starts quick,' she told the terrified girl. 'If you haven't got it now, you aren't going to.'

She looked at her uncertainly.

Barb tried again. 'Did the sick ones get ill quickly?'

The girl nodded.

'And once they got sick, they died really quickly too?'

She nodded again.

'What's your name?'

'Carol.'

'Right, Carol. We're the lucky ones who won't get the plague. But we will get sick if we leave the bodies lying around. Are there others who are still all right too?'

She nodded and looked up.

'Right. We need to get them together and organise

cleaning up and burying the dead.' She held out her hand to Carol again, and this time, she took it.

As they reached the next landing, they were met with a group of frightened-looking kids, who all seemed ready to push her down the stairs.

Barb took a deep breath. She had learned years ago that if you acted as if you were in charge, everyone behaved as if you were. 'Where's Matron?' She was met with a sea of blank expressions. 'Has anyone seen her?'

A boy stepped forward. 'She packed up and ran away just after Scratch died.'

Well, that figures, Barb thought.

'You're going to make us all sick,' a voice called from the back of the group, and again Barb felt the hostility rising.

'No. I'm okay. I don't know why, but I haven't got sick.'

They were still grumbling among themselves.

'Look, you've all seen how quick this disease is. If we were going to get it, we'd be ill by now.'

'There are some still sick.'

She felt her stomach turn over. So much for the disease having run its course. 'Where are they?'

'Upstairs.'

'Okay. I'll check them out in a minute. But in the meantime, we need to clean up this space and bury the dead.' She could see from the way the group were backing away that this was not a popular idea. 'You know they'll go bad, and we'll get ill from other things if we don't.'

One of the older girls stepped up. Barb remembered her as very quiet. Her name was Helen. 'What do we need to do?'

Barb smiled at her gratefully. 'Go down and get surgical masks and gloves for yourself and a couple of helpers. Then we need to move the bodies and put them by the lift. Someone else needs to be in charge of clean-up.'

An older boy called Will came forward.

Barb nodded gratefully. 'Go with Helen and get stuff from the cupboard: soap, buckets, cloths. Get groups working on each room, stripping the beds of the sick and taking the sheets down. Make a pile outside, and we'll burn them.'

'I thought you said we wouldn't get sick now.'

Barb hesitated. She was making this up as she went along, and it wouldn't take much for them to realise it. 'Do you want to sleep on those sheets?' she asked.

Will shook his head, and the looks on the other kids' faces showed what they thought of that.

'Better to be safe,' she added.

As the groups moved off, she braced herself to go up to the next level. Barb realised that little Carol was still clutching her hand.

Barb turned. 'Best stay here. Check they're all doing it right.' Carol nodded solemnly, as if either of them believed she had any chance of ordering the others around.

The smell on the next level was worse.

It had always been sweaty and nasty, but now it was also sickly sweet. Barb didn't need to go far to find out why.

There were no survivors up here, and no one had been well enough to look after anyone else. She felt the sickness rising and raced back down the stairs, taking gulps of the relatively clean air.

It might be better to burn the whole building down and start again.

She focused on calming down. Doing a quick head-count, she thought there must be less than half of the children left. Thirty or forty from about one hundred before the sickness. It seemed to have affected the younger children more. It would be hard to find somewhere for all these kids to live, so on balance, it looked as if they needed to make the best of it. She only hoped her plan would work, because otherwise, this was going to be much harder.

Time to try it out. She pushed the button of the lift, and with a juddering screech, it magically opened. She began to feel optimistic.

Wedging it with a chair, she indicated it grimly to Helen, who had returned with a couple of well-covered helpers. 'We'll take the bodies down in this.'

Helen raised her eyebrows in surprise.

'It's the best idea I've got, and if it works, it will make upstairs easier to deal with.'

She nodded. There really wasn't too much choice.

There were about seven bodies on this floor, and once they were loaded, Barb pressed the button for the ground floor and removed the chair. The door juddered as it shut, and there was a grinding sound from the lift shaft.

'Come on,' she called to Helen, and ran down the stairs to meet the lift at the bottom.

Slowly the door opened, and she grabbed a trolley to hold it again. She felt ridiculously relieved. Now they just had to hope their luck held out for the trips needed to the third floor.

36

Their luck did hold out regarding the lift, but it had run out for the thirty-seven bodies lined up outside, waiting for the trench grave to be finished. Looking around, Barb reckoned about thirty kids had either run away, and hopefully survived, or been taken by the scientists. As they'd worked, the youngsters had shared stories of sick kids being driven off in vans and not returning.

It had been a gruelling day, and she couldn't have done it alone. If there were children who refused to touch the dead, Helen and Will had cajoled them into digging the mass grave. There had been tears and angry words, but finally they had accepted they had to do a task, and chose to shovel dirt. A few had left, but for most, the unknown had seemed a worse option than what they were creating here.

Barb had been worried about how they would eat, but late in the afternoon, the usual grocery delivery arrived outside.

She walked up the drive and started to open the iron gate.

'Don't come any nearer!' the driver shouted. He had the

lorry doors open and was already piling food out on the ground.

'What are you doing? You can drive in, and we'll help you unload.'

'No way. I'm not coming in. I've heard about what's going on in there. In fact, I nearly didn't bring food. There can't be enough of you left to eat all this lot. Stop right there, or I'm off!'

Barb held up her hands and backed away. 'There are some ill, but most are all right. Okay, I'm not moving. Just leave the food.'

The driver started throwing the food out as fast as he could, ignoring Barb's shouts to be careful. At last he jumped down and stormed around to the driver's seat.

'Make sure you come back next week!' Barb shouted as he drove off. She wasn't convinced they would see him again.

She ran across to the food and started trying to sort it out to stop any more packages splitting. A bag of potatoes had burst, and some of them had smashed as they'd hit the ground. Vegetables were scattered around, and the few tins that sometimes turned up among the food were dented.

'Get a trolley,' she shouted down the drive, and soon some of the younger children came trotting along, pushing and pulling a trolley between them. They stopped and stared at the mess on the ground. 'Come on, get sorting,' Barb instructed, fighting back the tears of anger, and directing herself into the practical work of salvaging as much food as possible. It was just as well there were fewer to feed, but they would have to be careful how they rationed this lot, as she suspected things were about to get a great deal less predictable.

That evening, they finished burying the bodies in one

huge pit. They burnt the sheets in a giant bonfire, and all came out to watch the flames throwing shadows over the raised mound where the bodies lay. Some of the children cried quietly, thinking about their friends, including Barb as she thought of Scratch carefully placed in the middle of the grave with his arms thrown out wide, on guard and forever looking out for all his little people.

Barb left them all to look in on the two sick children upstairs. There had been no more deaths, but despite what she told the others, she wasn't convinced they'd seen the last of it yet.

37

One week on, things had settled into a new normal.

Barb sat at the desk in the room that used to belong to Matron. She could see why the old spider had set herself up here – you could watch exactly what was going on and who was coming and going. She'd never realised what a great spying spot it was. She watched Helen and Will organising things around the Bank, not quite coordinated yet, as they sent different children off to do the same jobs without consulting each other. She'd have to persuade them to talk more and agree what was the priority for themselves if this was going to work. The new Barb and Scratch, she thought, although neither had the same easy way with the younger kids, or the fun, playful spirit he'd had.

Pursing her lips, she felt the anger inside her, pulsing with her heartbeat and growing so that she could use it when the time came. She was going to get that girl that had caused all this trouble and pain. What had Vander been thinking? Or more to the point, had he been thinking at all? She had never liked him.

Although it was a hot day, she crossed the room to close

the window to block the smell of the fresh grave. It should have been further from the building, she realised now, but at the time, it was all they could do to get them out and buried. Besides, it was an unpleasant but important reminder of why she needed to leave soon. She had wanted to see things settle before disappearing, but they were as settled as they were going to get, and every day, that girl was probably spreading the disease and infecting more people.

There was a quiet knock on the door. Fix sidled in. It was an unimaginative name, but it represented him very literally. No one could remember if he was officially a resident at the Child Bank, but he'd been allowed to come and go for years, though where he went in between visits was a mystery. However, it suited everyone, as Fix found things people needed: objects, food, information. He had a knack for appearing when something needed sorting out, and vanishing when it all went wrong.

'Hi, Fix. I need you to do something for me.'

He nodded as if there had never been any doubt that this wasn't a social visit.

She hesitated. Would this put Fix in danger? Meanwhile, he looked around the room as if sizing it up.

'I need a gun. Something I can put in a pocket. Would you have any idea how I could get one?' She wasn't sure if she really wanted him to say yes or no.

He nodded. 'I could get one in exchange for the lollipops.'

'Lollipops?'

'Yeah.' He nodded earnestly. 'They're really hard to get hold of now. My supplier likes them.'

Barb hesitated. The lollipops had been there for many years, and they got given out in real emergencies, if a child needed to be extra brave. Would she be mean in exchanging this one small pleasure for her chance for revenge?

'Guns are really hard to get hold of. Ones that work, anyway. And you'll need ammunition too, so that will be part of the deal.'

I'm trying to get rid of a dangerous person here, she thought as she tried to justify it.

As she hesitated, Fix reached for the door.

'All right, all right.'

He stopped. 'I'll need payment up front for this one.'

She nodded. 'Come on.' She took the storeroom key, and they headed off. Barb had hoped to be less controlling than Matron, but she'd soon found out that a building full of kids could wipe out their entire food stock in a day with their grazing natures.

High on a shelf sat a tall jar, half-full of increasingly sticky lollipops. She reached up and pulled it down.

Fix opened a pocket, and they poured them in. She wondered how she'd never noticed what enormous pockets he had before now.

'I'll have it by this evening.' And he was gone.

38

Max was finding it hard to forget the pretty but strange girl who had caused so much commotion that day. She would probably have stuck in his mind anyway, she was so intense. It was the way she listened to everything as if it were important. Most customers barely looked him in the face and certainly didn't think he had anything important to say. She was different. And then there was the matter of a hall full of sick and dying kids. It had seemed that she was the only one to walk out of that unscathed. He shuddered at what might have happened to him if he'd investigated himself and not run away.

Running away was his speciality.

However much he tried not to think about his family, they crept back into his mind. He'd run from them three years ago, and it didn't get any less painful. He'd come to the city to get away from the isolation, but he was just as alone surrounded by people.

Was it worse to be lonely in a city of people or in a farm-house in the country?

When they'd questioned him about the girl, they'd told

him she was very dangerous, but would not explain in what way. She had looked harmless enough, but they wouldn't have a huge cordon around the centre and a stream of people in hazmat suits swarming all over the place way into the night in that case. Perhaps she'd been making a bio bomb, and it had gone wrong.

Anyway, his worst problem was that he'd been ordered off work for two weeks, had been told to remain isolated and report in if he had a fever. It was as bad as being back in the farmlands, and he would have no money and therefore no food in the meantime.

His stomach rumbled just to highlight the point.

Ironically, it seemed this girl had headed out towards his family home, where they had barricaded themselves all these years to stay safe. He wondered if they were still all right and, more importantly, if they were still vigilant against strangers and the dangers they posed. The hunger pains were nothing to the pangs of guilt he felt dragging at his conscience as he remembered that he had been the one to send her in their direction.

It couldn't be plague, could it? He'd been too young to remember the last outbreak – it had barely been during his lifetime. His parents had said it would never really go away, but then they had said a lot of crazy things, and he'd spent his childhood picking and choosing which ones were likely and which ones he wanted to believe.

He listened to his stomach rumble again and knew he couldn't stay cooped up in the flat, getting increasingly hungry.

It was unusual for Max to be free to wander the streets in the middle of the day, and by night he was generally too tired for a ramble. But without work, he decided to explore some new areas.

As he walked past the park, he took a detour further into it and enjoyed the greenery. He would never do this at the end of a night shift – too many strange people lurking in the wild undergrowth. The parks had become little forests with no one to tend them. They were more unkempt than his farm, where it was all cared for to produce the highest yield of crops. A few park areas had been ploughed up and used to grow vegetables, but the rest had returned to nature.

Feeling nostalgic for home, he climbed a tree high enough to get some sun on his face, and he wedged himself into a fork in the branches.

As he sat half-asleep in the warm nook, it was as if he were nine years old again. On a day like today, he had met his first outsider.

NO ONE CAME to the farm, or left the farm. The boundary wire was so effective it could have been a brick wall six metres high. At the end of the growing season, his father bundled up a portion of the produce and took it just beyond the boundary. The next day, it would be gone. Very little came back in, and what did went through a thorough and relentless cleaning process. When Max asked where it went, he was told 'the people' came to get it.

'You're better off not thinking about the people outside,' his father told him. 'They are full of disease. Dangerous. We send out food so they leave us alone; they stay clear so we can keep feeding them. They need us more than we need them.'

Often during these talks, his mother turned away or left the room. Once, Max had stormed out of the rant, bored with the standard lines, and had found her clutching a book of photos and crying. She'd put her finger to her lips and pointed to his father, and Max had understood this was not to be talked about.

His younger sister would roll her eyes at the talk of disease and pretend to suffocate and die on the floor, out of sight of their father, of course.

The day that Max met his first stranger, he'd been hiding up in an apple tree.

He was tired and had had enough of back-breaking fruit picking. So what if they got a bit mushy? Perhaps that was how he liked them. He'd picked about ten baskets of raspberries that morning, and eaten about one basketful.

In the distance, he could hear shouting; it must be his father calling him to do a job.

As he sank his teeth into an apple, he heard a cough. Beneath him, at the base of the trunk, there was a bundle of clothes. The clothes coughed again.

'Who's there?' he called down, sure it had to be his sister, Cissy, hiding too.

But the clothes slowly unfolded themselves and revealed a girl. About the same size as himself, but thinner. So thin he could see her bones pushing up through her skin. Her eyes looked enormous, and her hair was thin and balding in patches. She coughed again, into a cloth, and held herself tight as if in a freezing wind, although the sun still shone hot and fierce.

'Who are you?'

'I'm Sarah. Can I have an apple?'

Max was so shocked at seeing this girl that he dropped the bitten apple down to her. It fell to the ground, but she quickly scooped it up, and with a cursory rub on her coat, she bit into it hungrily. She swallowed chunks so fast that she was nearly choking on them, but she seemed unable to stop stuffing it into her mouth. Max was on the verge of jumping down to pat her back and stop her asphyxiating herself with apple pieces, but he hesitated as she pushed the core into her mouth and finally chewed.

'My dad's gone to ask for some food from the farm-house,' she said, indicating Max's home.

And then they heard it. The shouting. And then a single gunshot.

Sarah froze in terror. There was more shouting and two more shots, followed by a man's scream. She bent over and vomited up the apple in a neat little pile and then, seeming to recover herself, circled to the far side of the trunk, making herself as small and inconspicuous as possible.

Looking up, she put her finger to her lips in exactly the same way his mother did when she needed his collusion, and without thinking, he nodded.

The shouting was getting louder and nearer.

Max peered between the branches to see what was going on. He could see his father advancing across the orchard with his gun swinging around, looking for his target.

For a moment, Max thought his father might be looking for him in a fit of madness. There were tales of farmers stricken with a fever turning on their families rather than risking them falling sick with the plague, killing them all rather than suffering the illness. He clung onto the branch with both arms, scared of showing himself, sure that his father's paranoia had tipped him over the edge of sanity.

But then he shouted, 'I know you're there. Your father said you were out here. Come in and we'll talk.'

He was getting closer, still with his gun raised and ready to shoot.

'We have food in the house. Come out, and you can join your father for a proper meal.'

It was at that moment that Max knew that his father would not let this girl go.

His tone was gentle and his voice soft – exactly as it was before he slaughtered an animal for their meat. 'Come on, lass. I won't hurt you.'

Max wanted to warn Sarah. He wanted to jump down and protect her, or shout for her to run. But he didn't. He looked down as, lulled by his father's words, she stepped out.

He shot her.

Max clung to the branch, barely able to breathe. He was sure that if he made a sound, his father would shoot him too. Ringing in his head was a terrible question. Would it be worse to be shot by accident, with his father thinking that he was a stranger, or be shot on purpose to cover up what he'd witnessed? Death by paranoia or by malice?

His father had spent some time searching the orchard for anyone with the girl but, luckily, did not have the imagination to look up. Then he went to the outhouse where he kept a hazmat suit and returned dressed in it, carrying the body of a malnourished man. He dragged the man and Sarah to the edge of the orchard, just beyond the magical boundary, and then spent time bringing wood up from the back of the house. Sparing a little of his precious petrol, he poured some on top and then stepped back and lit the fire.

His father stood and watched the fire consume his victims. Max watched him.

Once it was clear that the fire was burning thoroughly and it wasn't threatening the nearest trees, his father turned to take the hazmat suit back. Max could hear him shouting for his mother to come and hose him down.

Max stayed in the tree until the fire had almost burnt

out and he was sure that his father would be safely inside and wouldn't see him coming back from the orchard.

Finally, he went home, because he had nowhere else to go.

'Where have you been, then?' his father fired at him as he came in the door.

'I was up at the pasture,' he replied. 'I heard some bangs. They sounded like shots.' He looked at his father's face to see his reaction.

'Vermin,' he said, getting up to leave the room. 'Vermin after our food.' And he walked out.

Max hadn't done much climbing after that, and went off apples too, much to his father's annoyance.

Eight years later, as he left the farm, his father's parting comment had been, 'Don't come back.'

'I won't,' he replied.

And three years on, he hadn't.

39

That night, the resurrected memory featured in Max's dreams for the first time in years. But now Sarah had the face of the girl at the station.

When he woke, it was with the heavy knowledge that he had to go back to the farm.

Maybe his father would be dead. Maybe not. Would his mother and sister still be there? There was only one way to find out.

It didn't take many minutes to pack a bag with a spare set of clothes and a water bottle. He hesitated before throwing in an old surgical face mask too. Nobody really used them in the city now, but it might be useful in the more rural areas, where the fears took longer to die.

He wondered if he was meant to tell the Facility people where he was going. They seemed pretty lax about the whole quarantine thing, but then that was to his advantage.

As a compromise, he decided to travel once the busiest time was over, so he had less chance of coming too close to anyone else.

Once he was on the train, it surprised him how fast it

was to reach the southern end of the line and return to his childhood home. In the city, it was easy to pretend that the farmlands were very far away, too far to visit easily. Not that he had wanted to, anyway.

40

Update.

        The trail has run cold.

You've completely lost her?

        At this moment ... yes.

What are you doing to find her?

        There are three likely stations where she might have disembarked, so we're working our way out from each one.

Are you thinking she has gone into the farmlands?

        Most likely.

In which case, she may well be dead. The inhabitants are more likely to shoot first and ask questions later. In which case, that's sixteen years' research finished in the time it takes to pull a trigger.

We have offered rewards for her return.

Only useful if you use shops. Most farmers use a barter system.

We could offer cows.

I doubt they would trust our cows. I wouldn't.

We'll get a lead soon, no doubt. Another body or two on a farm.

We may not know that has happened until a crop fails to show up.

41

Max approached the farm cautiously. Traps and tricks hadn't been his father's tactic – but things changed. He wanted a chance to talk to him before getting blown away. There was no sign of life.

Please let them be here, he thought.

He approached the farmhouse from the front, up the main track, which ran through the land where the largest harvests usually grew. There were crops in some of the fields, but they were small, almost overrun with weeds, a fraction of the usual planting. Every step filled him with a little more foreboding. As he drew closer, he could see how much paint was peeling from the window frames, and a few of the shingles clung tenuously to the roof. A big storm would cause a lot of damage. Had it always looked this shabby and he never noticed? No. In a few short years, the place had deteriorated rapidly.

The door to the farmhouse was locked when he tried it, which surprised and then saddened him. His mother had always been in and had the door on the latch. There had never ever been any need to lock the door.

Pressing his nose to the window didn't reveal anything

other than dirt inside and out, and he wiped a cobweb from his hair.

He was moving less quietly now, as the place felt abandoned and empty. At the back, the door was not locked. He pushed it gently and was about to step across the threshold when he felt something cold and hard press into the back of his neck.

'Don't move if you want to live.'

'Hello, Dad,' he replied as he slowly turned to face his father.

His father looked at him, stony-faced. *Just as well I wasn't expecting hugs and kisses*, Max thought.

'Better go in, then, if you're going,' he said, but he didn't lower the gun.

'Are Mum or Cissy here?' Max felt that he'd rather know now than face the evidence inside.

'Cissy died two years ago. Your mother not long afterwards.'

Max felt a rage of pain, and he wanted his father to at least look as if it upset him too.

'What happened? Did you shoot them?' he spat out.

Now his father lowered the shotgun. 'Of course not. Go in and we'll talk.'

Max's world was one big red angry wash. All thought of why he had come had gone from his head. 'I'm not sure I want to stay.'

At that moment, all he wanted to do was march away from the farm without a second thought. Or kill his heartless-bastard father. Or kill him, then march away.

Behind him the door opened from the inside.

'It's you again.'

He turned at the sound of a young woman's voice. It was the girl from the station, here in the house. He stepped in front of her, expecting his father to raise his gun again and shoot her.

'Move out the way.' His father pushed him aside. 'Are you all right, Mary?'

'Yes, thank you, Frank.'

'Don't just stand there,' his father shouted back at him. Max gathered his thoughts and walked into the kitchen.

'This is my son, Max. The one I was telling you about.'

Max wondered briefly what his father had been saying about him.

'Thank you for sending me here, Max.' Mary pulled a chair up next to him, and it was Frank's turn to look surprised.

'I didn't,' he replied defensively. Why had he sent her to this area? He would never ... would he?

He shook his head, unsure of what he'd been thinking. 'Did Cis get the Red Plague?'

His father's face darkened. 'No. Blood poisoning. She cut her finger and it got dirty. No medicine to touch it.' He looked towards the dirty window.

'Mum?'

'She gave up. Seemed no point going on.'

Max waited for more detail, but it was clear he wasn't going to get any. 'But you have. You've managed to go on.'

Frank shrugged. 'People still need food. Don't hit the quotas any more, but it's better than nothing.'

'And what about her? Mary?'

'She needed somewhere safe to stay. Couldn't turn her away.'

Max looked steadily into his father's face. 'I saw you that day.'

His father looked back at him. 'I know.'

He broke their gaze to look over at Mary. 'She learns

quickly, but she doesn't know much to start with. Guess she's been very sheltered. Even more than you and Cis.'

'Aren't you scared that she might have the plague?'

'I was never scared for me, Max.' He shook his head to show there would be no more tonight. He'd already talked more than usual.

'You'll have to fend for yourself if you want to eat. I'm no cook, and neither is this one.' He gestured towards Mary. 'I have to tell her what can be eaten raw or needs heating. No idea.' He shook his head and headed towards the door.

'I'm off to check on the cows. You might as well use your room. Mary's in Cis's.'

The door slammed behind him, and he was gone.

Max looked at Mary. 'They're turning the city upside down looking for you. A lot of people are getting sick.'

She gazed back at him with her extraordinarily blank look.

'They're getting sick and dying.' He jumped up, knocking the chair over. 'Don't you care?'

She flinched away from him and looked down at her hands, clenched together in her lap.

'I don't really know what to think,' she replied.

Max picked up a glass and threw it against the wall. Perhaps it was as well Mum and Cissy were dead. All those years being careful, and he'd sent this cold, infected woman straight to his home. Looking around, he saw that Mary now sat rigidly in the chair, not moving, barely breathing.

'Should I be worried?' he asked her coldly.

'I don't know,' she whispered. 'Your father has been fine. He bandaged my finger, but he still stayed well.' She held up her finger for him to inspect.

Rubbing his face, Max took a deep breath, trying to gather his thoughts. There was no point worrying about it at this stage. If they were infected, it was too late to do anything about it.

He walked into the pantry and was surprised to find it was still relatively clean and well stocked. This had clearly been his father's domain, though he'd never appreciated it. There were cheeses on the marble slab and various vegetables in bags and on racks. The main thing missing was baked goods. No bread or cakes, although there seemed to be flour and some eggs. He wasn't going to start baking tonight, but he could pull together an omelette.

Picking up the bowl of eggs, he carried it through to the kitchen and put it on the table.

'What do I do with this?' Mary held up an egg.

'You need to break it in here.'

Max watched with amazement as she took the egg and threw it into the bowl, smashing it. She laughed and picked up another one.

'No!' He took it from her and put it down. 'You can't eat the outside ... Well, I suppose you can, but it doesn't taste nice.' He got a spoon and fished out the pieces of shell.

He took another egg. 'Like this.' Cracking it smartly against the edge of the dish, he split it in two and dropped the contents in. 'Look, I'll do it. You watch.'

'No.' Mary grabbed another egg. 'I have to learn.'

'It'll be quicker if you watch,' Max insisted through gritted teeth.

'If you're not here, I need to be able to do it.'

Half an hour later, they finally had omelettes with only minimal amounts of eggshell in them.

It was probably the worst meal Max had ever eaten at home, but not the worst meal he had ever eaten since.

Bed was a relief after that.

42

We have a team ready to go up to Lakeside and find her.

No.

No? They are ready to go.

Unready them. I'm going to go myself.

Why?

I want to handle it.

Why?

Because I've got bored of waiting for you to.

We're nearly there.

No. I'm going. I'll let you know when to come. Otherwise, you are to leave it with me. And ...

Yes?

You don't need to let the Wuckers know about this. Don't worry, I will sort it out with them afterwards.

43

Marinda stood outside the Child Bank for a couple of minutes, weighing up the pros and cons of actually going in.

She wanted to get a sense of what had happened there, but there might be lingering microbes, and she couldn't deny she felt rather squeamish about that. In fact, it was rare for her to venture out of the Facility at all.

Let's hope the new vaccine is up to scratch, she thought.

She had a lot invested in the Bank.

Although it had higher powers involved, she had personally put a lot of her own money into this one. It seemed rather obvious that having control over the future workers was useful and generally profitable. However, if they all went and died, it was not such a good investment.

After taking a deep breath of relatively uninfected air, she went in.

It had the inevitable sickly smell combined with bleach. There was a rising aroma of something indefinable being cooked. The hall was cold and had a floor that was much lighter in the middle, where it had been cleaned, fading to a dark grey around the edges, where the cleaning mops clearly failed to reach.

'Hello. Can I help you?'

She turned to face the young woman who had come out of Matron's office. 'I'm looking for the person in charge.'

The girl looked incredibly pale and seemed to be upset at the sight of her. Marinda assumed this was the girl who had been with the victim who had brought the plague here. *It would be interesting to see what she divulged*, Marinda thought.

'That would be me,' the girl replied.

'Really?'

'Were you expecting someone different?' she challenged.

'Well, yes, I was. You aren't the matron I appointed to run my Bank.' Marinda smiled. 'Are you all right? You're looking a little off colour.'

'I'm fine,' she snapped. 'You'd better come in.'

Marinda marched past Barb into the office and sat down in Matron's seat behind the desk. Barb scowled and crossed her arms, but said nothing.

'Do take a seat and introduce yourself.' Marinda sat back and studied Barb, who was still standing in the doorway.

'My name is Barb. I was Matron's assistant and have been running the place since she left.'

'So, what happened?'

'Haven't you seen her? I thought she went to the Facility.'

'Hmm. I was just interested in your version. Besides, I've been a little busy dealing with another problem.' Marinda smiled again while thinking she'd never been required to look so amenable before.

Barb kept her face neutral, but her brain raced as she started to make connections. 'The kids got sick and she ran off.'

'How unprofessional.'

'Do you want a tour?'

Marinda shuddered. 'I don't think so. You seem to be doing well. Are the food deliveries still arriving?'

'Yes, though they won't come into the grounds.'

'I'll speak to them and see what I can do. Well, I have somewhere I have to go, so I'll be off.'

'Just one thing.'

Marinda turned back. 'Yes?'

'Was Matron being paid?'

'Matron was working off her indenture. She had a while to go yet.'

Barb took a moment to wonder how many years Matron had been working to pay off a childhood debt.

'Then I want the same arrangement.'

Marinda looked at Barb's shabby clothes. Why not? She seemed to be managing, and there was no one else lined up. Matron had become redundant.

44

Barb ran upstairs to watch Marinda leave.

As she took the stairs, two at a time, Barb realised that in her rush to defend her position she hadn't even asked for that woman's name.

She reached the window on the landing just as Marinda walked the last part of the long driveway. Whoever she was, she was from the Facility and either knew where Mary was, or would be searching for her too.

The timing was perfect. Fix had delivered the gun last night, so there was nothing to stop Barb following her.

She needed to find Helen and Will to give them the storeroom key.

45

It was the last train that evening before the power went off for the night, and it had very few passengers, and none who wanted to sit near each other or make eye contact.

Barb kept her head down but watched the woman's shadow as it moved down the carriage to the end. She took a seat near the door but with her back to Marinda. This was so much easier at night. She concentrated on staring out of the window into the darkness while really focusing on the reflection of her target.

The soft edges of the reflection made her look so like the girl she was searching for that it sent goosebumps up Barb's back and made her feel sick with anxiety.

She thought of the children back at the Bank and wondered if Will and Helen had managed to get them settled for the night. *No point worrying*, she told herself. *If this all goes wrong, they will have to manage on their own from now on.*

The swaying train made it hard to stay awake, and a couple of times, Barb caught herself tipping into sleep, only to jerk up awake again in a panic that she'd lost her target.

But Marinda was still there.

The next stop was the last one. Either this woman had arrived, or she, too, had gone to sleep. Barb decided to risk getting off first to look less like the stalker she really was.

MARINDA KNEW that she was being followed by that tatty-looking girl on the train who was making such a poor job of being subtle.

She imagined she had a weapon of some sort on her, probably a knife or maybe an old gun. Yes, she looked like the type that would know someone who could get a gun. Luckily, it was dark, and she probably couldn't use it.

She saw her get up to leave first at the last stop and tried to hide a smile, wondering how this wraith would try to remain hidden. The disquieting thought occurred that maybe she wouldn't bother following her and would just kill her quickly once out of the station. If only she knew who she was and what she wanted. An irritating idea scratched at her mind just out of reach. She looked so familiar, but why? Marinda flicked through the files in her mind, checking each point and trying to find the missing memory. Working backwards, it didn't take too long to find her.

The Girin Child Bank.

It was the girl who had taken charge after Matron had done a runner. She looked younger out here, without the children around her. Marinda struggled to remember details about her. She had seemed so unimportant and irrelevant before that she had barely bothered to listen to them at the time.

The thief who had taken the blank had come from the Girin Child Bank. He had been about her age.

It clicked into place. This girl's boyfriend, Snip or Snap

or something equally ridiculous, had brought the virus into the Child Bank. They must have had contact with Mary and the thief.

The girl had looked pale when they'd met. It hadn't been tiredness or illness, as she'd assumed, but shock at seeing Marinda. She had seen an older version of Mary arrive and been upset.

Marinda smiled to herself. She was following her because she wanted to find Mary and thought she would lead her there. Mary was the intended victim. It was good to know that she had a backup. Now she had to get everyone in place and light the match.

She chuckled and shook a matchbox in her pocket. She loved these old things, rare now but so pretty and useful. She would enjoy using these last ones on this adventure.

BARB PULLED BACK into the shadows as she left the station, and let Marinda walk past and along the road before starting to follow her again. She stumbled and caught hold of the gun as it bumped against her leg inside a pocket of her oversized coat. She wondered if she would really be able to use it when the moment came. She tripped again, stopped for a giddy moment to calm herself. She could taste bile in her mouth but realised it could be hunger as much as fear that was affecting her. She bit the inside of her cheek to focus.

She'd lost sight of the older woman, but the road only went in one direction between the hedgerows. The darkness enclosed her, and it was impossible to see more than an arm's length ahead.

Barb struggled to keep quiet and not fall, swearing at herself for not having brought a torch. Suddenly a flash of memory swept over her as she remembered the moment, as a child, when all the lights had gone out forever. She had been alone in the street and was already scared. Street lights and house lights had disappeared in an instant. The city had run out of energy, been switched off. It had felt as if everything had stopped. As if they had fallen off the planet and were floating in space.

She fell to her knees, numb to the cuts and grazes. The world had ended.

Eventually, she rallied, as she had all those years ago. Back then she had staggered into the nearest building and a different life. In time, some lights had returned; humanity had faltered but teetered on. However, now she decided it would be better to curl up in the hedgerow and wait for daylight. At this rate, she might easily walk into that woman and not know until it was too late. The ground was damp and prickly – she'd slept on worse.

MARINDA HAD FOUND the barn further along the road. She was fairly confident that her shadow-assassin had fallen back and stopped for the night, but she took a moment to pull together some scattered straw behind a long-abandoned vehicle. Once she was confident that she was well hidden, she settled down to doze through the night.

The corner of the matchbox pressed into her hip, and she leaned into it rather than shifting. She wondered about setting fire to the barn now – that would get things moving – but regretfully rejected the idea. Better to wait until dawn and be fully prepared. She still held the element of surprise.

46

Up in the farmhouse, Mary was awake. She still found the unregulated temperatures outside the Facility difficult to adapt to. She knew that there was spare bedding in the room next door.

Slipping along the landing, she was momentarily shocked to see a figure outlined against the window. 'I'd forgotten you were here. I wanted another blanket.'

Max struggled against the irritation that she would consider him the stranger in this house. 'Help yourself.' He turned back to the window.

'What are you looking at?' She joined him, squinting into the void outside. For a moment, she felt thrown off balance by the vastness of the black on the other side of the glass. It seemed deeper and darker than inside a locked room and reminded her vividly of the night she had stepped out of the Facility for the first time. Max caught her elbow to steady her.

He peered out to the silhouette down the lane. 'I thought I heard the barn door swinging loose, but it seems to be closed.' As he leaned back, he caught the fresh, soapy smell of Cis's pyjamas on Mary, and it evoked the memory of standing with his sister, looking out into the night and wondering what lay beyond. He'd often tried to make her go out after their parents had gone to bed and explore the world at night. She never would. 'Got what you needed?'

Mary nodded.

'Night, then. See you in the morning.' He dismissed her.

He watched her leave the room and hesitated before pulling the curtains across the window. Living in the city had made him jumpy. Tomorrow he would have to decide whether to go back or not.

47

Barb was the first to stir the next morning. It had been a horrible night of unfamiliar noises and unknown threats. It hadn't rained, but she was damp through from the morning dew and cold to her core.

She scrambled to her feet, alarmed to hear her joints rubbing together like unoiled metalwork. The hunger reminded her that it had been a full day since she'd last eaten. *You've got soft*, she thought. *Time was that you could go a few days without food.* However, she knew that was only bearable when her stomach was full of water, and so she looked around for something to drink. A nearby puddle looked muddy, but most of the sediment was settled at the bottom, so tentatively she got back down and took a few mouthfuls. The activity stirred up the soil, putting an end to that. Around her, there was dew on the grass, so she pulled up a handful and sucked on it. Then, finding that quite sweet tasting compared to the puddle, she chewed on it. Once all the moisture had been extracted, she swallowed the pulp. She'd eaten worse.

Stamping her feet and waving her arms around, she began to feel the blood move. *Time to go.* She had no idea how much further Marinda had gone or what would happen next, but standing around here wouldn't get any answers.

She felt for the gun in her pocket and for a moment was thrown into a panic when she realised it wasn't there. It must have fallen out in the night.

Retracing her steps she found it pressed into the hollow where she'd slept. She took the hem of her coat and hurriedly wiped the worst of the mud off. There was no time to clean it more thoroughly; she had to find the older woman.

Up ahead, the road curved to the right, so she crossed and skirted around the sharp edge of the bend, peering around to what lay next. The barn seemed to rise up out of the ground mist as if it were floating or coming in to land from the sky. Further along and slightly up the hill was the house. Everything was still.

She couldn't see Max and his father leaving the back of the house, with Max dragging his feet like a stroppy teenager being made to help with the chores.

Nor could she see Marinda finishing her regime of exercises after eating the rations she'd brought in her bag.

MARINDA HAD NEVER VISITED this farm but had enough dealings with food providers to know that all competent hands would soon be at work, doing the daily tasks that made even this run-down plot stagger on.

She pulled herself up straight into a stretch that lengthened her spine, before looking around to take stock. Grabbing hold of the broken rake in the corner, she started to pull the scattered hay into a pile. There were a few poles and boards lying around, which she stacked onto the top before throwing the rake on for good measure. She pushed the door ajar and peered out. The sun was truly up now, and out of the corner of her eye, she caught the movement of her stalker edging towards the barn.

Ready to go.

She took out the box of matches and ran her finger along the rough side, enjoying the shiver that ran down her back. She held it to her nose and inhaled the tang of all the matches that had been scraped and ignited on it. There were two matches left in the box. For a moment, she thought about saving one. No, she was feeling wild today. It was a two-match kind of day.

She took out the first and struck it. It gave her such pleasure to watch the sudden light flare and then settle to a flickering, lazy yellow flame. Ah, it was the simple things in life that made it all so worthwhile. She dropped it into the hay and, for good measure, lit the second and pushed it into the other side of the kindling.

The straw was old and tinder dry, so it guzzled the flame, taking hold quickly.

Marinda slipped out of the door and headed up to the house.

She expected Mary to be sitting or lying somewhere safe in there. It was unthinkable that she would be out on the farm, so now all she had to do was find her.

The front door was locked, so Marinda quickly walked around until she came to the back door and let herself in. The kitchen was empty and had two doors leading off it. She chose to look through the smaller door first, expecting a cupboard. As she pushed it open, she was smacked in the face by a large pan, which knocked her out cold.

48

When Marinda regained consciousness, she was tied to a chair.

Mary pulled her own seat up so they were sitting face to face. She leaned forward towards Marinda so that they were almost nose to nose.

Marinda's immediate reaction was to hold her breath. After ninety seconds, she had to exhale suddenly, which made Mary laugh but did not make her move.

'It's not funny. Please move back. I can't breathe properly with you pressed up against me.'

Mary moved back a few centimetres.

'More. Please.'

She edged back.

'More.'

Mary tilted her head a little. 'No.'

Marinda rolled her eyes. Mary had clearly learned some survival skills since her escape. She wanted to feel her nose and find out how badly it was damaged, and she gagged at the metallic taste in her mouth. A trickle of sweat or blood tickled as it crept down her cheek and hung as a drip on her chin.

'Have I seen you before?' Mary asked.

'I do know you, Mary. We've never met, but we are connected. If you've seen your own reflection, you'll know that you look like me.'

This seemed to be a strange idea for Mary to process.

'If you let me go, we could go and find a mirror to look in.'

'A mirror?'

'It has a shiny surface so you can see yourself in it. Let's go and look.'

Mary shook her head. 'I don't think so.'

Oh well, Marinda thought, *it was worth a try.*

'You're from the Facility, aren't you?'

Marinda hesitated. 'Yes.'

Mary expressed no obvious emotion at this news. 'Did you know I was there?'

'Yes. That's why I'm here. We've been looking for you. We were worried about you.'

Mary looked blankly at her. 'Did you ever wonder how I felt in that room?'

Marinda wondered how to answer, truthfully or kindly. 'No. I never spent any thought on it.'

'Why not?'

'I didn't think you really had feelings. No sentient thought. You were a human shell.' *Too harsh?* she wondered.

Mary stood suddenly, sending her chair flying, and left the room, to Marinda's intense relief. Being stared at by your doppelgänger was very disconcerting.

She soon returned with a small mirror in her hand and stood in front of the chair. She looked hard at Marinda, then gave herself the same scrutiny in the reflection. Her eyes flicked backwards and forwards between the woman and the image.

'What does it mean?'

'As I said, we're connected.'

Mary shook her head. 'Explain.'

'You're a copy of me. A clone.'

Marinda looked for any sign that Mary had understood this. *Of course she hasn't*, she thought. *She's a blank.*

'We took some of my cells ... part of me ... and made you. Mary, you are me. We are the same.'

49

Barb approached the house slowly. It looked so empty, but she had seen Marinda go in. She wondered if she could practise with the gun without being noticed here. Fix had given her basic instructions: 'Put the bullets in here before you need it. Take off this safety catch. Point it and pull the trigger.'

It sounded easy enough. She had put bullets in, and now it lay in her pocket. However, even with her limited knowledge of guns, she realised it would be too noisy. The moment had passed, and now it was time to use it for real.

She could see smoke coming from inside the barn and had spotted flames as she came past. It seemed clear that it was a diversion that Marinda had set up, and she could see distant figures higher up the hill and suspected the fire was intended to lure them away from the house. All the better for her. She dealt with enough children to know that if they set up a distraction, you went and looked in the opposite direction for the real event – in which case, the house was where the action should be happening.

She went around the back, following the route that she'd seen Marinda take, and then peered through the window. Inside she could see Marinda, and it was instantly clear that her plan was not going as expected. Marinda was tied to a chair facing the window, but there didn't seem to be anyone else around. She looked up and caught sight of Barb peering in and, instead of looking surprised, seemed to be expecting her. The thought irritated Barb. Cursing, she strongly considered turning right around and leaving her to whatever she'd got herself into.

Instead, she pushed the door open and gingerly stepped inside.

'She's in the other room,' Marinda hissed. 'Undo me and we can overpower her.'

Barb hesitated for just a moment, but that moment was long enough for Mary to come back in. They both realised Mary was holding a long, sharp-looking knife in her shaking hand. All of them took stock of each other, and Barb raised her gun towards Mary but couldn't bring herself to pull the trigger.

Mary stepped forward. 'You were at the flat.'

Barb nodded.

'They came to get us there. Vander said you'd sent them.'

'Scratch died after he met you.' The words caught in Barb's throat. 'He got really sick and died. They said someone had escaped from the Facility and was spreading the disease. It was you. You killed him.'

'I didn't do anything to him.' Mary seemed genuinely confused.

'I'm afraid you did, Mary,' Marinda said.

'Who is this?' Barb looked between them, so very, very alike. Only age separated them. 'Is she your mother?'

'My mother?' Mary looked at Marinda.

'I explained to you, Mary, I am not your mother.'

'You look exactly the same,' Barb said doubtfully.

'You could be my mother.' Mary looked at her wide-eyed.

'No.'

'Mums make their babies. You're sort of my mum.'

'You're my clone,' Marinda spat out. 'A medical clone.'

Barb and Mary both fell silent.

'I didn't think things like that were real.' Barb remembered the scary stories the children had told each other during the dark nights at the Child Bank. They usually involved tales of being accused of a crime, and then discovering that it had been an evil clone who was trying to replace you. This would be followed by days of insults, which would fly around the playground and quickly degenerate into fights.

'You're a clone,'

'Your mother was a test tube.'

'You're a test tube.'

'You're a test gone wrong.'

Barb shuddered. 'Clones aren't real.' She looked at both the women again and knew they were.

There were no mismatched features, nothing that could be explained as coming from the father. The upright hairs of Marinda's left eyebrow were perfectly reflected in Mary's. The shape of her chin, her nose, her ears were all aligned. Their hair fell along the same ley lines.

'I was made. Is that why you did all those experiments on me?' Mary asked Marinda. 'I bet mums don't experiment on their children and hurt them like you let them hurt me.'

'So Vander set you free,' Barb interjected in an attempt to get this conversation back again. 'Did he know you were infectious?'

Mary frowned. 'Vander was nice to me. He didn't want to hurt me.'

Marinda could see that Barb was sympathising with the blank. How sickening. How inconvenient. Barb's hate and desire for revenge was starting to slip away, and a twinge of pity was entering her voice. Marinda needed that anger to burn again.

She needed to light another fire.

50

Up in the fields, Max and Frank saw the smoke from the blaze below and immediately ran towards it. Once the panic that it might be the farmhouse had subsided, the fear that Mary might still get hurt took hold, and it was all Max could do to stay upright as he hurtled towards the fire, pulling away from Frank, who stopped short, overcome by a coughing fit.

Once Max reached the barn, he could see that the old wood was smoking rather than burning, in what looked like a badly arranged bonfire. With no one to tend it, it had fallen apart. Each small gust through the barn door fanned the glowing edges of the wood and puffed out smoke, dwindling embers imitating an inferno.

He pulled it further apart and stamped on the throbbing red heart of the heat, killing it quickly. He had just about finished as Frank staggered in through the door and took in the scene. 'That was set on purpose. It was never like that before.'

'Why would Mary set a fire?'

'I don't suppose Mary did. Do you reckon she knows how to light a fire?'

The men considered this uneasily and quickly turned towards the house.

'It was a distraction.' Frank put his hand on his son's arm. 'Slowly. We don't know what we're walking into.' He went across to the door frame and lifted down a key. 'Let's go in the front.'

51

Marinda looked at Barb. 'Please untie me and let me wipe my face.'

Barb hesitated.

'You have the gun,' Marinda pointed out.

'Untie her,' Barb told Mary, who scowled but did it.

Marinda reached for a cloth on the table and dabbed at her face. 'Your friend Vander knew what he was doing. They all had the dangers drummed into them during training and had to wear protective gear whenever they went into her room. They definitely knew the blank was contagious.'

'The blank?'

'The clone.'

'The human shell,' Mary added as she put her face in front of Marinda's. 'That's right, isn't it ... *Mother*?' She turned back to Barb. 'I didn't know I could make people ill. Not at first, anyway. I didn't really know much at all then.'

'So you really made her?' Barb asked Marinda.

Marinda gave a tiny nod.

'And she caught the plague?'

Marinda didn't reply.

Barb pointed the gun towards her. 'How did she get the plague?'

'She hasn't got it, exactly. She's a host.'

'What does that mean?'

'Her body is carrying the disease, but she isn't suffering the symptoms.'

'How did that happen?'

'We made her that way.'

There was silence in the room as Mary and Barb absorbed the new information.

'To experiment on her?'

'To find a vaccination to get rid of the disease.' A window rattled in the stillness between them.

'You're too young to remember what it was like at the start and when we had the first sweep. It was terrifying and unstoppable. The only way to stay safe was isolation, but it was almost impossible to be that isolated. We would have given anything to stop it. You have no idea what it was like when the disease was running rampant.'

'I got a pretty good taste at the Child Bank after your experiment got loose.'

'I never meant for that to happen.'

'But it did.'

Barb's heart rate was rising painfully. She had come here to get even with Mary for all the hurt she'd caused, but it wasn't so easy to kill in cold blood when Mary was just as hurt and damaged as the rest of them.

'With our work on the clone, we can find a way to vaccinate against the disease. It's our best chance of survival. If you get the Red Plague, you die.'

'No.'

'Sorry, but true.'

'No, it's not. Some of the children in the Bank have

come through. They were bad for a few days, but they are getting better.'

Marinda's eyes lit up. 'They actually had symptoms?'

'Yes. Mainly the older children.'

'The children of the early plague victims.' Marinda seemed to be thinking aloud. 'Some had the test vaccine or maybe contact in the womb, or as a baby or child ... I must see them.'

'So you can lock them up and experiment on them? I know you've already taken some of them from the Child Bank. What are you doing to my children?' Barb's finger tightened on the trigger of the gun. She was not going to hand her kids over to this woman.

'No, no. They'll be well looked after, get the best possible care, but we must investigate this. It could be the key to destroying this terrible disease. Listen, there have never been survivors before, and they will have natural antibodies.'

'There have been survivors before.' They all turned towards Max's father, who had come in quietly and was standing at the back of the room. 'You just never looked for them.'

'I would know if there had been survivors. I would have heard the stories.'

'Not if they kept low and didn't tell anyone.'

'Why would they do that? That's ridiculous. No one lived.'

'I did. Max's mother did.' He looked across to Max. 'Our families lived on neighbouring farms, and we were in and out of each other's houses all the time, helping each other out at harvest and busy times. We all got sick, every one of us. Me and Thea came out the other side to find all the others had died.'

He coughed a deep, rattling cough that rolled on for too long, robbing him of any breath to talk. When he took the cloth away from his mouth, it had blood on it.

'What rubbish. If you were immune to the plague, you wouldn't have it now,' Marinda stated.

'This isn't the plague. I had this long before any of you turned up. This is one of those old-fashioned diseases, like cancer or TB, which has been creeping up on me for the last six months. It's got a lot worse lately.'

'We do have some of the old drugs still at the Facility. If you come back with me, we can treat it.'

He laughed and coughed, then looked her in the face. 'I don't think so.' He walked over to Mary and gently took the knife off her and returned it to the drawer in the dresser. 'Never play with knives, Mary. You might get hurt.'

He turned to Barb and glanced at the gun. 'I need a word with Max. Keep an eye on her, and we'll be back soon.' He nodded to Max, who followed him out of the room.

52

Max followed his father into the living room and sat down. He expected his father to sit in his usual seat at the end of the table, but instead, he pulled out the chair next to him and sat. He put a large book on the surface in front of them. It was the one his mother had often clutched to her. He realised sadly that they had never even asked to look inside – it had always seemed too private and personal.

He opened it.

Individuals and groups smiled out from the pages. 'This was your mother's family.'

At the back stood a farmer with his hat pulled down so far on his head that his face was covered by the brim and shadow. It gave the strange impression that he had no head, but he was a big man, towering over two pretty girls in overalls. 'This little one was your mother. I was going to marry her older sister, Adele.' His finger lingered over the face of the older girl as if stroking it. 'We were just months off the wedding when everyone got ill.'

They sat for a few minutes until Max thought that

might be all he was going to say. As he shifted in his seat, it seemed to bring his father back again.

'When I got well enough to get up again, the rest of my family were all dead. I raced over to Adele's farm, desperately hoping they'd been spared, but they were all gone, except Thea. She was still really sick, but she was strong. She pulled through.

'We heard over the radio that it was wiping people out; it hadn't just been on the farm. We didn't mix much with the others, anyway; we'd just been unlucky. The vicar that was going to marry me and Adele had it. He had come out to the farm the week before to talk about the arrangements, and he must have passed it on then, when both our families were together.

'Thea always thought I was disappointed it had been her, not Adele, that survived. I always thought she blamed me for the vicar coming out to us and infecting us all.'

'Were you disappointed?'

He looked up, surprised. 'No. Obviously, I would have liked Adele to have survived, but not instead of Thea. We both loved her. She might have been dead, but I guess the memory of her was always sat there between us, and we didn't have the heart to move her.

'We were scared to leave the farm; we didn't want to. And it was inevitable we came together. I mean, we were lonely, and we were young. At first we didn't even know if anyone else was alive out there. The radio and television went off. No one came to visit. The world went quiet. We thought we were Adam and Eve, alone in the garden.' He smiled and chuckled.

'Well, eventually, we realised there were other people out there – they wanted us to keep giving them food, for one thing. But we decided that whatever happened outside, we would stay together and keep everyone else off the land. We agreed to send a share out to the others, but we didn't want them near us. We only wanted each other and to look after each other. Then, when you and your sister came along, it became even more important to isolate ourselves. We needed to keep you two safe. We couldn't have taken any more loss.

'We would have done anything to keep you safe.' They looked at each other. A girl hiding behind a tree trunk rose in their memories. 'I did do anything to keep you safe.'

They both were lost in their own thoughts for a moment.

'You must have known we'd want to leave at some point,' Max said, 'or at least find other people, find out about the world beyond the fence.'

'We didn't think about it. I guess we thought if we ignored it, it wouldn't happen. Then you left and your sister died.

'When Mary turned up and told me what had happened to her, well, it made me wonder if the farm had been no better than that for you.'

Max put his hand on his father's arm. 'There is no comparison. Yes, you kept us up here, but we knew there was another world out there. We saw the sky and the fields. You let me go.'

'You didn't give me much choice.'

They sat in silence.

'I did want you to come back.'

'I know.'

'I'm going to sort this mess out, Max.'

'It's not up to you to sort it out, Dad.'

'No, but I won't be around much longer, and you've got lots still to do. I hoped ... your mum and I both hoped that the fact we'd both survived the illness meant that you and Cissy would both be immune too. We were too scared to test it out, but if it came to it, we hoped you'd be saved, like we were.'

'Well, I haven't got sick yet.'

His father nodded cautiously. 'Be careful.'

Max put his hand on his father's arm. 'If you go back with Marinda, she could make you better again.'

His father shook his head. 'She's lying. They don't make those drugs any more, and if they do, they wouldn't waste them on an old farmer. I got lucky – I've had a life here with your mother and you kids. Most people of my generation never got that far. Your turn now, Max. If we let that woman go back, with or without me, she'll take Mary back and probably round you all up too.'

'What are you going to do?'

'Take her up to the old farmhouse, your mother's family's old place. I'd like to see what's left of it again, anyway. Adele and our parents are buried up there, with your mum and Cissy. Time to go and pay my respects.'

'I'd like that.'

His father shook his head. 'Not you, Max.'

'But I want to come too.'

'You need to sort out what you're going to do here. Get on and look after the living.'

'But what will you do up there? How will you survive on your own in a run-down old farmhouse?'

'Max, you've got to stop worrying about it. That side will be dealt with. I've lasted long enough down here on my own. Focus on what's going to happen to the rest of you.'

53

In the kitchen, Marinda rapidly regrouped her thoughts. She could see Barb was wavering – all that mothering of the brats in the Child Bank had made her a soft touch for a sob story. She needed reminding about why she'd come here.

'I hope your friend' – she racked her brains desperately – 'Scratch didn't suffer too much.'

'Shut up. Don't talk about him.' Barb waved the gun in Marinda's direction. 'He'd have hated you.'

Marinda held her cool. 'Why, Barb? I'm the one who kept the food coming to the Child Bank. I wanted you all to be safe – you were the children I never had.' She forced a smile, aware that this attempt at warmth was well beyond her comfort zone.

'I'm your child, *Mother*.' Mary moved uncomfortably close to her again.

'You are *not* my child, and I am *not* your mother,' Marinda spat back at her.

Barb laughed. 'We can all stop pretending you did it for love, I think. We were just there to feed your workforce.'

A horrible thought crossed Barb's mind, and the blood

200

rushed to her head, making her dizzy. She struggled to keep her voice even as she asked it. 'Have you been experimenting on any of the children you took away?'

Marinda thanked the stars that she could answer this one truthfully. 'No, of course not. They wouldn't have been at all suitable. Who knows what diseases they already had?'

'Well, as long as it was for all the right reasons.' Barb's voice was dangerously quiet.

Marinda took stock of the situation. She knew that she was going to have trouble talking her way safely out of this. Chit-chat had never been her thing, and it wasn't a skill she was going to master in the next half hour.

Mary had withdrawn into herself. She stood by the sink, looking at them, but with a glazed, faraway look that suggested her mind was somewhere else. *Or just switched off*, Marinda thought. It was the familiar look she had worn at the Facility. *Good*. She'd stay there like that for hours if left. A perfect target.

Barb was looking decidedly more animated. Quite twitchy, in fact, which was never a good look in someone waving a gun around. Marinda reckoned that her lack of sleep and the drop in adrenaline after the initial confrontation was making it hard for Barb to focus on the situation.

Having slept reasonably well on the straw, eaten and kept calm, Marinda knew she was in far better shape than these children. She needed to get Barb to come closer.

'I can get us out of here,' she whispered.

'What?'

Marinda used her best exasperated look and jerked her head to indicate Barb should come closer, and reluctantly Barb moved in. 'I can get us out of here. You don't think the men are going to let us go, do you?' She was pleased to see uncertainty cross Barb's face.

'Our argument isn't with them.'

'No, but I know these farmer types. They don't trust anyone.'

'Well, in your case, that's sensible.'

'They won't trust you either,' she shot back. 'They're making a plan in the other room, and that plan is probably to get your gun and get rid of us both.'

'They haven't killed her.' Barb glanced across at Mary.

'No. Well, they have to have some entertainment. Look at her. She's young, pretty and not going to put up a fight.' Barb barely had time to register the comment before Marinda seized her chance. She had had enough and was now leaving with Mary, dead or alive. *This thing had better be loaded*, she thought with annoyance, as she lunged for the gun and swung it around to hit Barb on the side of the head. Barb cried out and staggered under the momentum of the blow from the older woman, but she held on and for a moment the two women wrestled for control, their bodies pressed together.

The gun was between their heads, pointing at the ceiling. Barb clutched it tightly, resisting Marinda's efforts to pull it away from her.

Mary did not move.

From the other room, the men heard a cry, a crash and a loud explosion.

54

As the noise of the blast rattled out the windows, Max and Frank leapt up scattering photos in their scramble for the kitchen. Max reached the door first.

He barely heard his father call out a warning to slow before flinging it open. Immediately he stepped backwards, bumping into Frank, his hand across his mouth in shock, trying to stem the smell and the bile rising in his throat.

Frank pushed him out of the way to get in and check what had happened.

Mary was standing by the sink, staring blankly ahead.

'Check Mary's all right!' Frank shouted back to Max. She looked shocked rather than injured – the blood splashed across her front seemed to have come from the bodies on the floor. Max crossed the room to her, turning her away from the horrific scene.

'Take her out, and leave the door open to let some air in.'

As Frank bent down to untangle the injured women, he heard a groan. Someone was definitely alive, but who? His hand slid on the blood-spattered skin as he tried to grasp an arm and roll the top body off the other victim. He steeled himself and wiped away gore from a face to find Barb beneath. Her face, hands and shoulder were peppered with scraps of metal. Each wound oozed a trickle of blood, but not enough to explain the sheer quantity covering her.

He hauled the dazed girl up and sat her on a chair.

'What happened?'

'She leapt for the gun.'

'And you shot her.'

'No, no. We were fighting for control. I pulled the trigger and it didn't work, but then she got it and fired and ...'

Frank looked down at Marinda. A large splinter had pierced her neck. 'The gun exploded,' he finished for her.

It had been an old, ropy-looking specimen and clearly hadn't been looked after.

'It could have been me.' Barb's voice was shrill, and at the thought of what might have been, she bent over and retched onto the floor, tears and snot pouring down her face.

Marinda's wound had stopped bleeding so profusely, and Frank wondered if she could be saved if he tried. It was a passing thought, as he knew in his heart that even if he could resuscitate her, he didn't want to.

Frank stashed this ugly truth deep inside where feelings didn't reach and turned to the more straightforward turmoil in his kitchen. Barb's sobs had given way to silent shaking, and he turned to pat her shoulder gingerly, conscious that the girl was covered in shrapnel that could still give her an infection. Carefully taking her elbow, he helped her up and led the way outside to sit beside Mary.

Mary looked up. 'Are you all right, Barb?' she whispered.

'I don't know,' she replied numbly, looking down at the cuts and layer of blood.

'We'll find out as we sort this all out,' Frank said gruffly. 'Max, come and help get the bathtub down. We need to fill it and clean up Barb.' He turned Mary's face up to the light and gently wiped a finger over her cheek. 'Looks like you escaped the shrapnel. Come on, we need to get that out of Barb first. We all need to do this, come on.'

He set Max and Mary to boiling water and filling the old bathtub he had brought outside. It was better out here than in the horror of the kitchen. That would have to wait until they'd sorted Barb out.

Fetching a bottle of whisky almost forgotten in a cupboard, he poured Barb a glass. 'Drink it all down.'

Once he was sure she had drunk it all, he went and got one of the best cotton sheets from the cupboard. He set Mary to work. 'Cut it up. Like this.' He showed how to snip and rip the sheet into lengths and left her concentrating on that. Finally, getting the meagre first aid kit, he got out the tweezers and fetched a bowl.

'We need to get her clothes off and put her in the tub, then start getting out the shrapnel.'

'I can't. We can't strip her. It's not right.' Max stammered.

'Get a grip!' Frank roared. 'Embarrassed is better than dead and she can't stay in these nasty clothes. Now pass the scissors. It will hurt less to cut them off. She'll fit Cissy's or some of your old stuff when we're done.'

Max watched his father very gently cut and pull away the shivering girl's blood-soaked clothes. He soothed with gentle words and gave her more alcohol. Max had a flash of memory, a broken arm, blood from a bump to the head, his father holding him, comforting him, treating him. Dad had always dealt with the medical stuff and mended them. Finally, Barb was sitting in the hot water, and they could see the mass of metal shards in her skin.

'Can't we just wash her and leave them?' Max looked with horror at the task.

'Got to get them out. Could get infected.' At that, Frank turned away, racked with a coughing fit. He held out the tweezers to Max. 'No good me coughing over her. You'll have to do it.'

Max shook his head in horror.

Frank shook them at him. 'You have to. I'll go clean the kitchen. Anyway, your eyes are better than mine.'

As they stood at an impasse, looking at each other, Mary leaned across and took the tweezers. 'I can do it.' She stared them out. 'It's like the Facility.'

Frank shrugged and watched as, carefully, she eased out the first piece from Barb's skin. She held it out, and Max put a bowl beneath to catch it. Once he'd seen her pull some tricky bits from her neck without difficulty, Frank left them to it. The wounds weren't as bad as the amount of blood suggested, but he had seen the outcome of sepsis on his daughter, and he didn't want to see it again.

Frank felt very weary and out of breath. Suppressing another bout of coughing, he went around to the outhouse to get some sheeting and a shovel. He'd planned to kill Marinda once he got her up to the old house and away from the kids, and while it had saved him the task, he would have done it a lot more cleanly. When he'd been Max's age, it would never have occurred to him that he would end his life a murderer, nor that he would dispose of bodies with such a hardened heart.

. . .

AS DUSK CAME AROUND, Frank returned from cremating Marinda's remains by the perimeter. He found Barb tucked up in Max's bed. They'd done a good job of cleaning her up, and Mary had even put a couple of stitches in the deeper wounds. Max had set up a chair and a blanket next to the bed and was preparing to watch over her.

'She'll be sore tomorrow. Painkillers ran out long ago, so she'll have to manage with the rest of the whisky and some willpower.' Neither raised the fact that they were also running out of alcohol to wash the wounds.

Downstairs Mary was now trying to make an omelette by chasing some broken eggs around the pan. 'It looks a bit lumpy.'

Frank shrugged. 'It'll taste fine, I'm sure.'

As he looked around the kitchen, he caught a few smudges of blood on the cabinet doors and the unmistakable smell of meat past its prime. He decided he would eat his eggs in the front room for a change.

55

Statement from Blatt Meds

Maureen Posts will be taking up responsibility for the running of Blatt Meds with immediate effect. Dr Marinda Blatt has decided to take an indefinite leave of absence from her role as director of the Facility and Blatt Meds.

Dr Blatt had recently been working with the Child Bank, which she has so generously sponsored over the years. Unfortunately, at this time, the Child Bank is currently under quarantine after what appears to be an outbreak of food poisoning, which has claimed a small number of lives.

A member of staff from the Facility recently absconded but has now been located. It is thought that maybe these recent difficulties have made Dr Blatt wish to take some time away, and we wish her well and a speedy return to our company in the future.

'That all looks to be in order. Please send it out.'

'Shouldn't we be asking if anyone has sighted Dr Blatt?'

'That would suggest that we don't know where she is.'

'But we don't.'

'They don't need to know that. There is absolutely no need to cause any further panic. I'm sure Marinda has her reasons for ... taking a leave of absence.'

'What if she's in trouble?'

'If she's in trouble, I'm very sure she will manage to get herself out of it.'

'She might need our help.'

'Did you never meet Dr Blatt?'

'Yes, briefly.'

'Did she strike you as the kind of person who needed anyone's help?'

'No-o.'

'Well, that's because she isn't. She won't want it. She won't thank you for it. The best you can do is keep the Facility running smoothly, ready for her return. Any other stupid questions? No? Well then, get on and release the statement, please, and I'll get on with keeping Dr Blatt's work going. Don't slam the door on your way out.'

56

Max held Barb gently. After a couple of weeks, he knew her body intimately, and more importantly, he knew where each wound was scattered and how deeply it hurt. In fact, he probably knew them better than Barb did, for whom the pain merged and moved in ways she didn't understand.

Max knew where to put his hands to lift or roll her and where to stroke to soothe and distract her. He knew all her new wounds and most of her old ones too.

He traced a finger along one of the faded silver scars that criss-crossed her back like delicate netting. He found it hard to imagine anyone doing this to a child. She shivered and wriggled.

'You'll have to go back to sleeping in the chair if you're going to tickle me,' she complained. But they both knew that wasn't going to happen. One night, when Max could hardly stand from the exhaustion of farming and caring, he had collapsed into bed beside Barb and finally slept, and they had shared a bed since then.

He had held her as she'd sobbed for Scratch, and when she'd shaken with pain when the alcohol had run out. He had woken her when she screamed out during dreams of burying endless piles of children in a pit, and he had whispered his secrets in her ear, unsure whether she heard him or not.

Through the darkest nights, they had done whatever they could, whatever it took, to comfort and console each other.

The past two weeks had healed the outward scars and changed some of the inward ones. Max was certain that he would never know another person so thoroughly, both body and mind, and that thought made him light-headed and scared.

But then he was tired of being scared, and he was tired of being alone.

He gently pulled her over to him and looked at her sore, scarred face. It embarrassed her more than all the personal acts he'd performed for her over the past weeks, and she turned away. He drew her nearer so she couldn't escape his gaze, and leaned in, touching his lips gently to her skin between the angry cuts scattered across her nose, her cheek and her neck. She relaxed and returned his kiss as he reached her mouth.

He ran his hands down the curve of her back, feeling her thin body against him.

'Omelette.' The door burst open with Mary carrying a tray.

'Oh.' Barb staggered off the bed, gagging, and ran for the bathroom to be sick.

'She's moving faster,' Mary commented. 'Max, you've got no clothes on. You'll get cold.'

Max pulled the sheet around him, gripping it angrily. 'Mary, you should knock on the door before coming in.'

'Yes, Frank keeps telling me that too, but it's hard to

carry a tray and knock on a door. Anyway, I don't really understand why.'

'Because sometimes people need private time alone.'

'You weren't alone,' she pointed out, putting down the tray. 'Shall I see if Barb's all right? She seems to be sick a lot at the moment.'

It struck Max that Mary was right in her observation, and it irritated him that she had spotted it. 'No. I'll go.' He picked up a robe and, joining her in the bathroom, wrapped it around her. She smiled weakly and went to the sink to rinse her mouth.

'Are you okay?'

'Yeah.' She turned to face him. 'It's the egg. If I never eat another egg again, it'll be too soon. Please can you take it out and open the window?'

She joined him back in the room, and he went to pull her back down onto the bed.

'No.' She put her hand up and sat on the edge of the mattress. Then, looking at his confused expression, she patted next to her and took his hand as he sat down too.

She ran her fingers over the new calluses on his fingers.

'Are you okay?' He put his hand over hers, holding it still. 'What's the matter?'

'I'm worried about the children back at the Bank. Now I'm getting better, I need to go and look after them.'

Max felt all his happiness sliding away. 'You're not well enough yet.'

'I am, Max. They might need me there.'

'I need you.' He closed his eyes, frightened to see her reaction to this open admission that he wanted her so much.

She kissed the tear that escaped down his cheek, and he opened his eyes.

'They need me in a different way. They might be starving or in danger.'

Max started to talk, but she interrupted him.

'I have to go and see. They might be fine, but I have to know if they are or not.'

He held her gaze. 'I'll come too.'

Barb sat quietly for a moment. 'Your place is here. The children need me, and the farm needs you.'

The salty tears stung her wounds, but they still hurt less than the pain in her chest. 'We'll find a way to sort this out, but I have to know what has happened to the children.'

Max got up and wedged the back of the chair under the door handle, and this time, she let him pull her back onto the bed. For once, they both ignored the cuts, thinking only that their time together in this room, shielded from the wider world, was coming to an end.

57

When they'd told Frank about Barb leaving, he'd insisted that they needed to go to the top fields to see something before she went. The day after he'd cremated Marinda, he had collapsed and spent a week delirious with fever. With Barb panicking whenever she saw Mary, it had been obvious how they should split the nursing. He was weak but back on his feet and determined they should make the walk.

Max and Barb made it to the top of the track first, both hot and carrying the warm clothing they'd set off in. The old, overgrown road was a longer route but less steep than the path straight up the hill. Max knew the old farmhouse was around this last bend, but wanted to wait for Frank and Mary to join them so they could approach together.

They sat on a large stone to catch their breath, comfortable with their silence. Max moved around to sit behind Barb, and she leaned back against his chest. He kissed the side of her neck and wrapped his arms around her body. She tilted her head back, and they both soaked up the rays of the sun on their faces.

Even with their eyes closed, they could tell that Frank

and Mary were near from the pants and moans. It was unclear who was helping who. Mary had never experienced such a lengthy amount of exercise and was almost crying with exhaustion.

'Sit down for a minute and catch your breath.'

Frank waved Max away. 'I've been sat down long enough. Just let me stand a minute.'

Mary lay down dramatically on the ground, groaning. 'My legs are going to drop off.'

The others ignored her.

'Right, let's go.' Frank set off again.

Max offered Mary his hand and pulled her up, and they fell in behind Frank, allowing him first sight of the house. As it came into view, they all stopped.

'It's huge.' Barb had imagined another house like Frank's, but it was more like a small country manor.

Frank shrugged. 'Thea's family were very well off, and they had a lot of staff. For all the good it did them in the end.' He turned and looked out down the next valley. 'This is their land too, though it will need a lot of work to get it producing again.'

He pointed to some small cottages down the hill. 'Those are some of the farm workers' houses. Again, it will take some work, but they could be used as well.'

Barb looked at him. 'Sounds like you have plans.'

He smiled. 'You need to bring the children here. They can all live in this house to start with if they share rooms, and then, as they get bigger, we'll renovate the cottages. I can teach them about the farm and pass that on. It'll all be wasted if I go and die without training others to follow.'

'What about me?' Max asked indignantly. 'I know about the farm, and I'm assuming this will all be mine when you do go.'

'Of course, but it's too much for one person, Max. We got by, but maybe getting by wasn't the best way to do it.'

Frank patted his son's back.

'Don't make the mistakes I made. If you settle the children up here, you can bring the place back to life again. And you'll be together. Barb doesn't need to go away, and you can raise your own children here.'

Barb blushed and turned away as Frank looked at her.

Max couldn't help grinning. He held out his hand to her. 'What do you think?'

She nodded. 'I think it's a great idea.'

'Is this our new house?' Mary asked.

Frank nodded.

Mary let out an enormous scream that made them all jump, and ran towards the door.

'Oh, Lord.' Frank hobbled after her. 'She'll go through the floor or do herself some damage. Come back, Cissy!'

Max hugged Barb. 'It'll need a lot of work. Looks like some of the windows need fixing, but we can do it together.' He squeezed her tight, making her wince. 'We can be together and safe.'

Barb watched Mary wiping a clean circle on the inside of one of the upstairs windows and pressing her face to it.

'Your dad keeps calling Mary "Cissy".'

'He slips. She reminds him of her. Makes him think of happy times. It's harmless.'

They walked towards the house hand in hand.

'This is perfect.' Max pulled her along, and she tried to look excited, but she wondered if she was the only one who questioned if they would be safe with Mary living in their midst.

Max thought she'd been asleep or too drunk to remember all those nights he'd confessed his anger at his father for shooting the outsiders, but she had heard and she remembered. He assumed she would be upset and angry at the story. He assumed she would think Frank had been wrong to go to such extremes to keep his family safe, but it was his assumption that was wrong.

58

Barb stepped carefully across the branches and then shuffled her way through the leaves that were starting to fall from the trees. She smiled at the noise they made and stopped to kick a particularly deep pile around for a couple of minutes.

She laughed aloud and carried on.

It was good to be alive and free to please herself. It had taken a lot of arguing to make Max let her come alone, but finally he'd accepted that he could get a lot of work done on the house and farm in a day and it was a more productive use of his time.

She picked some flowers along the way for Scratch's grave and thought perhaps she should think of planting some permanent flowering bushes on it. He would have liked that.

As she approached the edge of the woods and the grounds of the Bank, her happy mood began to evaporate.

Something felt wrong.

There were no children outside.

Everything was ominously quiet. She took a detour to place the flowers on the grave. It was lower and less smelly.

'I haven't forgotten you, Scratch. Hope you still have my back,' she whispered.

As she reached the front door, Barb was paralysed by a feeling of sickness in the pit of her stomach. She swallowed and took a deep breath before mustering her courage. She pushed the door open and listened.

Nothing.

She took five slow steps and stood in the middle of the hallway before calling out.

'Hello?'

Behind her, Matron's door opened.

'Hello, Barb.'

Luckily, she was able to look surprised without too much effort. 'Shaw.'

She went over to him and put her arms around him.

He stepped back to look at her. Taking her chin in his hand, he turned her face from side to side, inspecting the angry red scars from the explosion.

He took a finger and ran it over a particularly raw-looking one. She clenched her teeth and refused to flinch from his stare or his touch.

'I thought you ran out on me, Barb.'

She forced a smile. 'No. When I heard Vander had escaped, I went after him. He's dead now.'

Was he dead? Mary thought so, and Barb no longer had the stomach for the chase.

Shaw kept her gaze.

'Where are the children?' Barb tried to sound casual.

'Being useful. They're out getting food. The supplies stopped.'

'Even the babies?'

'They're at the top. Their crying drives me crazy, but I can't hear them up there.'

'Have you been waiting for me?' she asked in an attempt to appear playful and lighten the mood, but she felt the chill of his icy stare.

'No. I've been busy. I thought I'd run this place for a bit.' He was serious.

He pulled her towards him and started to unbutton her top, inspecting the scars across her shoulder as he went.

Then it struck her. He had failed to get Vander and Mary. She had asked him to do it and not fully disclosed what he was getting into. He'd got all excited about being a hero and being with her, and it had fallen flat. He had been made to look a fool and had made the Wuckers look incompetent. She had set it all up, and then she'd disappeared.

This role, looking after a bunch of children, was his punishment by the Wuckers. His fall from grace.

She was going to be made to suffer for this.

'I'm glad you're here,' she tried. 'We can make this our home together.'

His anger showed through as he ripped the last of her buttons and pulled the shirt off her back with her hands trapped in the sleeves. He twisted it, effectively tying her hands behind her, making it uncomfortably tight.

'I never wanted to have to come back here.' He ran a hand over her back, checking for scars while holding the shirt in one fist, keeping her trapped. He turned her back to look at her arms. 'I hated this place when I was a kid. Did you realise that?'

She shook her head and pursed her lips to stop herself from whimpering as he caught the edge of a scab on her shoulder while he explored her injuries.

'No. You were too busy making happy families with Scratch to see how miserable I was.'

She felt paralysed, like a rabbit caught in the killer stare of a stoat.

'I'm surprised you even knew who I was, Barb.'

She started to talk, but he pushed her roughly backwards, and she stumbled against a wall with no arms free to balance.

'Do you remember when I broke my arm?'

She shook her head unhappily.

'I was climbing a tree to get you the first red apple of the season. Do you remember visiting me in the hospital wing?'

She was determined that she wasn't going to cry.

'No?' He pressed her against the wall, leaning on her and crushing her arms behind her. 'No. Because you didn't. You wasted your affection on that joker. I've had lots of time to remember those joyful days while I sat here waiting for you to come back, Barb. It's amazing what you recall when surrounded by the smells and sounds of your past. All the ghosts come floating out of the woodwork.'

'It will be different this time, Shaw,' Barb whispered.

'Yes. Yes, it will. Because now I'm in charge, and you're not going anywhere.'

Barb wondered if Max would come looking for her when she didn't come back, but she realised they might just assume she'd decided to stay away. Even if they did want to find her, they didn't know where the Child Bank was.

'I guess you don't remember why I used to hang around you all.'

Barb shook her head uneasily. Scratch had always joked that Shaw had a crush on her, but thinking back, it was beginning to dawn on her that there was something more to it than that. He took a step back and looked her in the face with his ice-blue eyes. He was still wearing his Wucker uniform, but he'd lost weight over the last few weeks, and it was crumpled and creased as if he'd been sleeping in it. His face looked thinner, and he was unshaven and had thick red stubble. With a gasp, the second revelation of the evening hit her and knocked the breath out of her.

'You're Vander's brother.'

'Half-brother. Yes. I guess we always took after our fathers. At least, when we were kids, we must have done.'

'He never said.'

Shaw grunted. 'So ... you killed my brother?'

Barb froze frantically, trying to decide whether to continue with her lie. 'I didn't realise ...' she whispered.

Shaw turned and raised his hands up against the wall and leaned in on them. He was taking deep breaths to compose himself.

'I need to go and get some things from the place I've been staying at.'

'Really?' He turned and folded his arms.

'Yes. Clothes,' she said, pointedly looking at her ripped shirt.

'Okay.' He moved back and leaned against the door frame.

Flustered by his ready agreement, she struggled to untangle herself from the shirt, shaking out the twists and putting it on again. She fastened the remaining buttons and tucked the ripped bottom into her trousers. He seemed too calm, too in control, and she was unable to read his mood. It seemed that everything that she'd thought she knew about him had been wrong, and nothing seemed clear any more.

'I'll be quick,' she promised as she backed towards the door, afraid to turn away from him.

He smiled. 'When you come back, perhaps you'd like to meet our latest deposit.'

She nodded distractedly, getting ready to go.

'She's got an unusual name.'

Barb stopped.

'She's a scavenger called Beal.' He walked over slowly, enjoying her look of horror. 'You had a little sister called Beal, didn't you?' He twirled her hair. 'She looks just like you. In fact, she looks a lot better than you. You're not looking so good, to be honest.'

'Can I see her?'

'No. I don't think so. Maybe when you get back. I mean, you're not going to be long, are you?'

She shook her head. 'How did you find her?'

'She was among the scavengers that got infected by your little friend. She was very ill but is on the mend now. She will be so glad to see you. I've been taking special care of her, just for you, Barb.' He laughed a bitter laugh.

She thought of her secret and put her hand to her stomach. Would it make him soften towards her or make him angrier? If she told him now, he might never let her leave.

Just as she was coming to a decision, he lost patience and grabbed her by the arm and marched her to the door. 'Off you go, then. Don't forget to hurry back for your sister.' He pushed her roughly down the steps and slammed the door behind her.

Barb paused for a moment, then stumbled down the road, and once she was out of sight, she collapsed against a tree and sobbed until she felt she would never cry again.

59

Barb had run and limped back to the farm and had been in such a state by the time she arrived that it took a while to get the story from her.

'They've put a Wucker in charge. Not just any Wucker. His name's Shaw. He was meant to get Vander and Mary, but they messed up.'

'They came to the flats, but we escaped,' Mary whispered.

'Yes, it was him. So they've demoted him. He's mad, really mad, because he hates the Bank. He grew up there.' Barb took a breath and hoped no one had spotted the gaps in the story. 'I have to go back.'

'Not yet. We'll plan this.'

'No, I have to go back now. He's got my sister, Beal.'

Mary gasped.

'He's lying,' Max said grimly.

'What if he isn't?' Barb shot back. 'I don't think he has enough imagination to make that up. He looked so confident. He knows he has a hold over me.' She turned to Mary. 'You met her. He said she was at that hall you infected. What did she look like?'

Mary flinched but closed her eyes, trying hard to remember Beal. It seemed like another lifetime, and she had no idea how to begin a description. 'She looked like a girl ...'

'Did she look like me?' Barb shouted, as she banged her hand on the table.

Startled, Mary opened her eyes and looked at her intently. 'I ... I think so.'

Barb swore and got up to march around the kitchen.

'There can't be many girls called Beal. Realistically, it probably is her, Barb,' Frank reasoned. 'But we don't know if he has her at the Child Bank, and ...'

Barb looked at him.

'We can't be sure she's still alive.'

Barb sat down and picked at a rough edge on the table.

'I have to go back and find out. We need to save her, and we need to get the children away from him too.'

'We'll all go.' Max took her hand, but Barb sprang back.

'No. Just me.' What if Max found out that she'd told Shaw where to find Vander and Mary? What if he found out what she had done to make Shaw go?

She pressed her hands to her eyes, trying to stem the tears of fear and anger. 'He said to go back alone.' She'd figure it out.

'Shaw isn't going to let any of them go without a fight,' Max pointed out.

'No,' Barb agreed quietly.

'So you can't fight a Wucker.' He faltered. 'I mean, I don't think any of us can.'

'We have to do something.'

'But who here stands a chance against him?' Max looked around. 'Seriously, who is going to win against a Wucker? Dad is not well enough to even get there, let alone

225

fight a fit young man, and you're still injured and don't have a good record with guns.'

'You'll have to do it,' Barb said bluntly. Perhaps if Max shot him, she'd get away with it. He need never know the whole story.

'Barb, I really want to help you and the kids, but I don't think I can.'

'You're just going to abandon them?'

'No. I just don't know that I can point a gun at a man and shoot him in cold blood. I ... I can't touch guns.'

'Then get angry!' she shouted.

'I don't think I have it in me to kill.'

'I do.'

They all turned to Mary, who had been sitting quietly, listening. 'I have it in me to kill. I don't mean to, but I've killed more people than all the rest of you put together.'

They all thought for a moment.

'That might be so, but you haven't done it on purpose. How are you going to take him out?'

She shrugged. 'I think it might be our only option. I'm your best weapon.'

'It's a bit unpredictable,' Max said uneasily. 'Shaw might be immune to you.'

'He won't be immune to her attractiveness,' Barb said thoughtfully. 'If nothing else, you might be able to distract him to allow us to overrun the place.'

'I don't like it,' said Frank. 'You don't know what you're up against.'

Mary shrugged. 'That's been true from the start. I've managed so far.'

The others all looked at each other miserably.

'You might be relatively unscathed, but others haven't been so lucky,' Barb pointed out tightly.

'What's *unscathed*?'

'Untouched.'

'I don't think I'm unscathed.'

'Right.' Barb looked at her. 'It's you and me, then.' Perhaps she could get rid of both of them.

Max spluttered, 'Of course I'll come too. I just don't want you having any illusion that I'm going to be any good in a fight.'

'Maybe if I give you all a bit of training before you go, you'll stand a better chance,' Frank offered. 'But it'll have to be tomorrow. It's getting dark now.'

'But we have to get back there. Weren't you listening? Shaw's a monster. If I don't go soon, he'll hurt someone. He'll hurt Beal.'

'I reckon you have a day's grace. He'll get a little jumpy, but it's worth being prepared,' Frank insisted.

'One day,' Barb said. 'We can't leave it any longer than that.'

60

At around two in the morning, Max gave up trying to sleep. He'd drifted off a few times, only to wake suddenly at the sight of an emaciated young girl being shot to death in the orchard. He thought of all the violent arguments he'd had with his father as a teenager when he'd refused to train with a gun, and they had ended up back there anyway.

He crept down the stairs, avoiding the steps that creaked, and went into the kitchen to get a glass of water. He started when he saw a figure looking out of the window.

'Hi, Mary. I didn't hear you come down.'

'Hello, Max. This dark is different from the dark in my room.'

He joined her to look out of the window. 'In what way?'

She thought for a moment. 'It's shinier. And spottier.'

He laughed and choked on the water he was drinking. 'Spottier?'

'Look.' She grabbed his shirt and pulled him forward to look out of the window and then ran to the door and threw it open. 'Look at all the spots,' she declared, pointing to the sky.

Max followed her out. 'They're called stars.' He shook his head, frustrated by his inability to explain. He and Cissy had loved looking at the night sky.

'Did your sister look at the stars?'

He was shaken by her mentioning Cissy as he thought of her. 'Yes.'

'Do you wish your sister was here?'

'Yes, I do.'

'I wish Vander was here too. I think he would have liked this.'

Max put his arms around her and gave her a hug.

FROM UPSTAIRS, Barb watched them sadly.

She went back to bed and lay there. She didn't want to know what they were doing outside together. She twisted in the bedclothes, trying to convince herself that she didn't care if Max and Mary were attracted to each other. If Shaw told Max about her visit, he wouldn't want anything to do with her again. Max still couldn't forgive his father, and Frank had acted in defence of his family. What she had done had been pure fury and revenge.

She forced herself to think of Scratch but was alarmed to find it was difficult to hold his face in her mind.

Eventually, as she finally began to sink into a restless sleep, she dreamed of a man leading her along the road, but when he turned, it was Shaw, not Scratch, that was holding her hand.

61

F rank was up early and had checked and cleaned three shotguns by the time the others came down. He surveyed their dark-circled eyes and sluggish movements.

'You lot are going to be no use at all.'

'Thanks, Dad.'

'You can't mess with these things.'

'We don't want to,' Max pointed out.

They looked at the weapons, and they brought back horrible memories for all of them.

'Eat some breakfast and join me up at the field,' he ordered, gathering up the weapons and leaving them to it.

Thirty minutes later they all trailed up the track. Barb had set her jaw into a determined scowl. Max looked thoroughly miserable. Only Mary had a bounce in her step as she swung her arms and admired her yellow cardigan.

'Take one each,' Frank instructed.

Barb and Max stepped up and picked up the weapons.

'And you, Mary.'

'No, I'm not doing it.' She smiled.

'Yes. Everyone has to do it.'

'No. I'll watch.'

'Mary ...'

'Frank.' Her voice was steely. 'I don't need a gun. I will watch.'

'Let her be. Come on, Frank. Let's do this,' Barb said.

She was shaking as she tried to forget wrestling with Marinda, but it was hard as the barrel of the gun pressed against the soft scab of the wound Shaw had poked just the day before.

Max wasn't much better as he jarred his shoulder repeatedly because, try as he might, he couldn't stop the tension in his body.

After an hour, they took a break.

'It would be less tiring and stressful to walk there myself and shoot him,' Frank announced in frustration.

They had mostly missed their targets, although Barb had caught the edge a couple of times.

'Perhaps we can just frighten him.' Max was shaken by his lack of ability. Despite hating the idea of using a gun, he had assumed it would be easy and he would be good at it.

'I don't think he'll frighten that easily,' Barb replied glumly.

Frank did frighten that easily though, and now he wondered if he was about to lose his only son again. 'I really think I need to come with you.'

'No.'

Before the men had a chance to argue about it, Mary intervened. 'When I escaped from the Facility, we did it at night. Everyone was asleep, and it made it hard for them to see us.'

They all thought about it.

'Shaw must have to sleep,' Max pointed out. 'Does he have helpers, or is he alone?'

'He was alone as far as I could tell,' Barb admitted. 'But if he is asleep, then it's likely that the children will be too. We'll have to wake them up and get them ready. The power will be off for the night, so it'll be completely dark.'

'But you all know the Bank better than he does.' Frank was clutching at straws.

'The sound will travel more,' Barb said.

'He won't be able to see us to shoot,' Mary offered logically.

'We won't be able to see him. It could be a bloodbath, 'cause he won't care if he shoots us all,' Max fired back. 'Maybe we'll shoot better in the dark,' he added bitterly.

Barb laid a hand on Max's arm. 'To be honest, I don't think we're going to get much better in half a day, and it's just putting off the inevitable. We'd be better off getting this over with. If we set out now, we'll get there tonight as it gets dark, and we can choose our moment to go in.'

It was decided.

They picked up their weapons and started the walk down the hill back to the farmhouse. It was a bright, sunny day.

'I'll start getting the house ready for our guests,' Frank said. 'Max, come and give me a hand with the top shelves.'

They walked up the stairs to Frank's bedroom. 'Pass down all the bedding. Doubt it will be enough. Better get the older kids to bring some bedding with them. We'll have to see if we can go back for any of the supplies later.'

As Max moved to the door, he grabbed his arm. 'Max, I know you don't want any killing, but this Shaw guy ... he won't just let you walk away.'

'I know, Dad.'

'I mean, if you get away and he's still alive, even if he's wounded, he's not going to just forget it. He might come here alone, or he might go and get his Wucker friends to come after you. Sometimes you have to give things a definite ending, not leave loose ends.'

'You want me to be a murderer? Like you?'

'I would never wish my nightmares on you. Believe me, I dream of that girl every single night. But I don't want you looking over your shoulder every day for the rest of your life, wondering if Shaw is going to leap out at you. If you don't do it, then Barb or Mary has to. One of you has to finish it.'

Max stood and looked at his father for a moment. 'I know.'

62

There was no talking as they left. Each of them gave Frank a hug before turning to go. They had agreed to time their arrival as the sun went down. It would give them a little light to see what was happening, but it would mean they wouldn't be hanging around too long.

Barb decided to approach through the wooded area to give them some cover and somewhere to sleep if they did decide to wait until morning to act.

They walked at a steady pace, each caught up in their own thoughts.

Max wondered what would happen to Frank if they didn't return. He was still angry with him, but they'd spoken more in the last few weeks than they had in all the years before he'd left.

'What colour is this?' Mary pointed to a bush.

'Green.'

He had started to believe that they could make a relationship again, be like a father and son should be.

'What about this one, then?'

'Green.'

The thought of leaving Frank alone so soon was painful, particularly as he was sure that Frank would kill himself rather than slowly fade away once he thought they were dead.

'But this is different. What colour is this?'

'Green.'

'That makes no sense.'

'They're different shades of green.'

Mary shook her head.

He wondered what life would have been like if he hadn't witnessed his father committing murder, and whether he would have stayed on the farm. Could events have taken a different course and Cissy and his mother be alive too?

Barb thought of Beal. Did Shaw really have her? Was she safe?

'This is a different colour. What is this one?'

'That one's red, with some orange.'

Would Beal be happy to see her? What had her life been like after Barb had gone to live in the Child Bank?

Mary fell behind, frustrated at Max and Barb for failing to take her questions seriously. As they travelled on, there were more red leaves, and they were different shapes, wider and flatter.

Barb recognised the nest she had made on the night of her escape. They were near.

'You have to be quiet now, Mary. We're getting close.'

Mary huffed and kicked leaves around in annoyance. She wanted to point out that she hadn't been speaking to them for the last ten minutes out of anger, as a protest at their inability to give a sensible answer to her questions.

'Let's settle here until it's really dark,' Max whispered, and Barb nodded her agreement.

They put down their weapons and lay down to rest before their attack. Their lack of sleep the night before had taken its toll, and unintentionally Max and Barb easily slipped into unconsciousness.

MAX WOKE to feel the cold muzzle of a handgun being pressed against his forehead.

'Evening,' said a young voice.

Barb woke instantly and reached for her shotgun, but it was no longer there. She looked across and saw Max's predicament and stayed very still. Her shotgun was in Fix's other hand, giving him an off-balanced look that was worrying.

'Hi, Barb,' said the voice at the trigger end of the gun.

'Fix? Oh, thank God. Fix, give me that. He's a friend.' Barb held out her hand.

'Sorry, Barb. Can't do that. Your man Shaw has paid me good money to watch out for you and make sure that you don't creep up on him. Now, I know that, technically, you were all sleeping, but I reckon as soon as you woke up, you'd have started that creeping.'

'Fix, you can't go helping Shaw. He won't be good to you all. He's mean and angry.'

'To be fair, Barb, he's mostly angry with you, not us so much. As for mean, well, Matron was mean, and we survived her for long enough.'

'We've come to take you all back to a farm. There's loads of green land, and we can grow fresh food and have a good life there.'

Fix thought for a moment and then shook his head. 'To be honest, I don't think I want to live on a farm, Barb. I'm too much of a scavenger. All that hard work doesn't sound better than what I've got here.'

'No one would be keeping you there. We'd need someone to go and do the deals, selling the extra and getting us things we can't grow. Come on, Fix, put the gun down.'

'Could you at least move it away from my head?' Max suggested. He could feel the pressure of the metal digging into his skin.

Fix took a step back but kept the gun pointing at Max's head. 'Don't do anything stupid. Sorry, Barb. Business is business.'

'Hello.'

'Gaaaah!' Fix fell, and the shotgun fired, narrowly missing Max. 'Where did you come from?' he screeched.

'Calm down. She's with us.' Barb leapt forward to check Max was unhurt, and he clutched her to him, trying to slow the uncontrollable shaking that had overtaken him.

'How many more of you are there hiding around the place?' Fix swung his gun around, now convinced that every shadow was a new person about to jump out at him.

'There's just the three of us,' Barb tried to reassure him.

'Who are they?' He waved his gun between Max and Mary.

'Max's father owns the farm, and this is ... this is Cissy, his sister.' Barb squeezed Max's arm to keep him quiet and gave Mary a warning stare.

'I'm—' Mary started.

'Let me do the talking, Cissy. Leave her alone, Fix. She's just a kid, never been off the farm.'

He looked at her curiously. 'Get over there with them.'

Mary recognised him as the boy who had seen Vander pulled from the river, but Fix didn't seem to have made the connection. Several weeks of sun and fresh food had given Mary a tan and filled out her face, so she no longer had the fragile translucence that made her so obvious before.

'Er, Fix.' Barb looked at the handgun nervously.

'What?'

'Have you used that gun at all?'

'I can use it,' he replied defiantly.

'It's just, that gun you gave me sort of exploded. We might all be safer if you just put it down.'

'I'm not an idiot,' he replied, wide-eyed.

'It's true,' Mary said. 'That's why Barb looks so disgusting. We spent hours picking bits out of her.'

'Thank you, Cissy,' Barb cut in loudly. She unconsciously put her hand to her face and wondered if she was really as disgusting as Mary had said. She had avoided mirrors since the accident.

Fix went to push his handgun into his waistband. Then, thinking better of it, he dropped it to the ground and kicked a pile of leaf litter over it.

He collected the other shotgun and swung it over his back. 'Where's the other one? Three people, two guns?' he asked.

'Told you, she's just a kid. She didn't have a gun,' Barb replied.

'That true?' Fix asked her.

Mary was a bit confused about which bit of the story he was asking about, so she kept her mouth shut and just nodded.

'Right, let's go, then.' Fix waved towards the Bank.

Max got up and pulled Barb to her feet, and they set off.

Barb found that she was still holding on to Max and was wondering how to separate herself from him before Shaw saw them. It was easy enough though, as he flinched every time Mary stumbled on the rough ground. 'Go help your sister,' she said loudly so Fix would hear. It was probably for the best, anyway. It gave the big-brother story more credibility. She had no idea if Shaw wanted her back out of desire or revenge. Neither prospect was a happy one.

Max heard Barb stumble along behind him and felt miserable. Mary was now his sister, which was fine by him. He'd thought her beautiful from the start, but in a cold, distant way. It was a beauty you didn't need to touch but could look at from afar. But Barb. Barb was real. Barb made his heart hurt.

They came to the open space in front of the Bank. Before they reached the door, it opened, and Shaw stood there.

'I heard a shot in the woods. Were there more of them?'

Fix shuffled his feet. 'Er, no. Just letting them know I mean business,' he said brazenly.

Shaw had seen enough frightened new recruits to know when one wasn't quite telling the truth, but Fix seemed to find lying easier than telling the truth. Besides, he had Barb and her friends with a gun trained on them, so he was willing to let it go.

He opened the door wider and stepped aside. 'You'd better come in, then. To my office, Fix.'

They walked past him into the hallway. He stood for a moment, listening and looking carefully in the shadows before shutting it firmly and locking it with the key from the bunch attached to his belt.

Mary hadn't been that bothered about Max supporting

her through the woods, but once she stepped inside, the smell hit her, and she was glad of his hand on her arm. If her eyes closed, she would have thought she was back in the Facility. The air held the sharp tang that sat on top of, but didn't completely mask, the foul body smells underneath. Both smells were so much stronger here.

She felt nauseous and leaned on Max to stop herself falling over.

Barb tried to ignore them and focus on charming Shaw. *Concentrate*, she thought, *or we'll all be dead.*

The office wasn't large, and Barb felt that the desk seemed to be closer to the door than before, giving Shaw lots of space behind it and them very little to stand in. It must have taken a huge effort to shift it, but although Shaw looked lean, he clearly still had the muscles he had built as a Wucker. There were no chairs except the large, worn seat behind the desk that had briefly been hers but was now Shaw's.

'Glad to see you back, Barb,' he said solemnly.

She fixed what she hoped was her most winning smile. 'I said I'd come, Shaw.'

He smiled back. 'Indeed.'

Barb desperately wanted to ask about Beal, but although she knew he knew that was why she was here, it didn't do to make it too obvious.

'We're all very tired, Shaw. Shall we go and find some-where to sleep, and talk tomorrow?'

He went through the pretence of looking like he was thinking about this suggestion. 'I think we can at least do introductions now, Barb. Who are your friends?'

Barb tried to calculate how loyal Fix would be to Shaw and how much truth she needed to tell. 'Well, I told you how I was tracking Vander.' Next to her, she felt Mary flinch as she heard the name, and she immediately regretted that she hadn't discussed this with them beforehand. 'He went to a farm out of town.'

They were so pressed together that she could feel Max tighten his grip on Mary. She hated herself for it, but she hoped it was to warn her to be quiet rather than out of affection.

She pressed on, but carefully. 'That's how I know he's dead.'

Barb glanced at Mary, but she was slumped against Max with her eyes closed.

'So who are these two?' Shaw was tired and impatient.

'They were living on the farm. It used to belong to their parents.'

'Brother and sister?'

Barb nodded.

'Names?' he asked directly of Max.

'Max and M ... I mean, Cissy,' he replied, and instantly cursed himself. They were meant to be Max and Cissy. He could feel an angry heat from Barb and saw her glance at Fix, who was leaning against the wall, only half-listening.

Barb could tell that Fix had spotted the error. Although he still slouched as if he couldn't care less, his eyes were open wider, and he was giving Max and Mary a long look in the light of the office. It seemed Fix would keep this to himself for the time being, no doubt mindful that it gave him a small sliver of power over them.

She realised Shaw had asked another question. 'What?'

'So why are they here?' he repeated impatiently.

She paused and Max stepped in.

'The farm's too hard for just me and my sister. She's not so strong, and we wanted somewhere safe to come and live. Barb thought we could be useful here.'

Shaw looked at Barb and wondered why he'd ever been so obsessed with her. He was tired and couldn't help wondering if this was really worth all the effort. What did he have left now? He'd still be climbing the promotion ladder at the Wuckers if it weren't for Barb. He didn't want her any more, but she'd ruined his life, and he couldn't just let that go.

'What makes you think it would be safe here?' he asked with what he hoped was a suitable level of menace.

Shaw was startled when Mary laughed. He stood up and came around the table towards her. Max pulled her closer and tried to square up to him. Shaw wasn't any taller or stronger than farm work had made Max. He was, however, one hundred per cent more armed, and as he crossed the room, he put his hand on his revolver. The Wuckers had let him keep it. This was no bent-up artefact bought on the black market but a clean, functional weapon. No one in the room was under any illusion that it hadn't been used before and that Shaw wouldn't be willing to use it again.

He grabbed Mary's arm to pull her away from Max, who resisted until Mary, fed up with being in the middle of a tug of war, shook them both off.

'What's so funny?' Shaw demanded.

She stood up straight and looked up at Shaw. 'You're right. Nowhere's safe. Max thinks some places are, but I don't. That's what's funny.'

Shaw couldn't stop looking at this girl. 'You seem to have a better understanding of the situation than your brother.'

Mary held his gaze. 'I do.'

'Are you ill? Why are you flopping around?'

'I don't like the smell. It's foul.'

It was Shaw's turn to laugh, but he laughed alone.

Barb and Max exchanged an uneasy glance.

'Okay, Fix, Barb's right – it's late and they do look tired. Take these two upstairs and lock them in separate rooms.'

Fix pulled himself up off the wall. 'There aren't enough rooms, boss. I could put Barb in with Beal.'

'No. Put these two in together, then. Not with Beal.'

'Please, Shaw ...'

'No.' He swatted Barb away.

'What about her?' Fix waved at Mary, clearly not trusting himself to use her name.

'She can stay here. I have a room at the back that is surprisingly free of the foul smell.' He turned to Mary. 'It's much more pleasant than up there, and I'd like to talk to someone who seems to appreciate my sense of humour.'

Max stepped forward. 'No, you can't—'

Shaw moved swiftly and hit him around the head, bringing him to the ground. 'You don't get to decide. I'm in charge.'

Barb grasped Mary, hugging her.

'Don't worry, Barb,' Mary said. Then she whispered, 'This is what we wanted, a distraction, yes?'

Impatiently Shaw pulled them apart. 'Stop panicking. I won't hurt her.' Hands grabbed Barb, pulling her away and pushing her out of the room. She staggered as Max bumped into her, and she saw he had blood pouring down his face from a cut on his forehead.

'We need a dressing,' she told Fix, but he scowled at her and waved his gun around.

'I don't know what you're up to, but I covered for you. It had better not come back to bite me,' he hissed.

They went up to the fourth floor to a set of rooms that still had locks. They went past the first room, which was shut, and into the second. Fix slammed the door, and the lock turned. The only light came through the small window in the door, and as Fix walked away, he took this with him, leaving them in pitch-blackness.

Barb leaned Max against a wall and started to feel around the room with her foot. She shuddered as she pushed against debris that seemed to move on its own, and she used her fingertips to guide her around the wall. Gradually her eyes adjusted, and she realised there was the faintest grey light coming in through the bars at the small outer window. There had once been glass in the frame too, but that was long gone, and the early autumnal night was bitingly cold in these early hours before dawn.

She found the bed, which had a thin, stuffed mattress, and thought it might be best that she couldn't see what state it was in. She brushed her hand over it to dislodge any rubbish, then felt her way back around the room to get Max.

He had slid down the wall, and it took all her energy to get him to his feet and support him back to the bed. He lay down. Next, she tried to feel how bad his head wound was but became scared by how much blood there seemed to be. She slipped her jacket off to remove her shirt and then quickly put her jacket back on again, zipping it up to try to retain some heat. Folding up the shirt, she felt for the wound and pressed the shirt against it. She was alarmed to feel warm liquid already soaking through, so she pressed harder, ignoring Max's complaints.

Soon it became clear that she couldn't stand like this all night, as both the cold and exhaustion had begun to take their toll on her. It was a single bed, and her attempts to roll Max against the wall were unsuccessful, so she tried to climb across him but found there was not enough space on the far side and ended up lying across him. His arms came around her, and she was relieved to feel they still had strength, which suggested that he wasn't as badly injured as she'd feared.

They drifted in and out of sleep, trying not to roll off the bed and shivering from the dropping temperature.

63

Shaw listened to the slow, grumbling progress as Fix took Barb and Max upstairs, before turning to Mary. 'Right, Cissy.'

Mary was looking around the room and didn't respond.

He sighed. 'You aren't really Cissy, are you?'

She smiled. 'No. Though Frank likes to think I am. Cissy was Max's sister, but she died.'

'So who are you?'

'I'm from the Facility. I'm Mary.'

'You were with Vander?'

'Yes. He got me out.'

'Got you out?'

'I was trapped there. He got me out.' She smiled. 'He rescued me.'

'So you're what Vander stole?'

She nodded.

'I thought he stole some of the virus.'

Mary's face clouded over, and she shook her head.

Shaw sighed a deep sigh and massaged his temples. *Vander, what did you do?* he thought.

He knew he should return her, but then Vander had

risked everything to get her out. He owed the Facility nothing. He had no illusion that they'd locked Mary up for her own good or her best interests.

He stood up. 'It's late. There's a bed through here. I'll sleep in the chair.'

Mary looked at him doubtfully.

'It's all right. I won't hassle you. Go through and get some sleep.'

He let her go past and then sat once more. Perhaps he should try to stay awake anyway.

As the night wore on, his head drooped, and finally he succumbed to his exhaustion. He didn't hear Mary get up and leave the back room, nor detect her sidling past him on her way out of the office.

Before she left, she watched Shaw gently sleeping, slumped in the chair, and smiled.

He looked so much calmer and happier when his eyes were closed and his face was relaxed. He also looked a little less like Vander. She reached across and stroked his hair lightly with her fingertips. She'd been so glad when they'd met and she'd realised she could be with him. It was like she'd been given Vander all over again, and this time, she wanted to keep him.

64

A hand shook Barb, nearly sending her to the ground.

The lamp was on the floor, throwing a ghostly light around the room, but outside, it was still dark.

'If you want to go, you have to do it now,' Mary whispered.

Barb rolled to her feet. 'Are you all right?'

'Yes.' She started to walk away.

Barb grabbed her arm. 'Really?'

Mary gave a little laugh and shook Barb's hand away. 'Yes, of course. You heard Shaw. He hasn't hurt me. He wants to look after me. Come on, he'll wake up again soon.'

'We have to get the others, the children.'

Mary shrugged. 'Do what you need to do. I'll go back to Shaw.'

Barb saw she'd brought a second lamp, and she lit it now before heading back down the corridor.

'But you've got to come with us.' She chased after her. 'You can't stay here.'

'Why not?' She looked puzzled. 'I'm staying with Shaw.'

'He'll be so mad tomorrow when he finds everyone gone. You have to come with us. If you're still here, he will hurt you.'

Mary shook her head. 'He won't hurt me. He might want to hurt you, but not me.'

'Mary, you don't understand.'

'No, Barb. You don't understand him. Stay. Go. It's up to you. I'll help you find the children, but after that I'm staying. Here. Fix will help you.'

Fix stood before them. He grinned tentatively. 'So what's farming like, then?'

Before Barb could let rip with her thoughts, they heard a small voice in the still-locked room. 'Who's in there?'

Fix held up a key and put it in the lock. He turned it and opened the door.

Barb gasped and put her hands to her mouth.

'Hello, Barb. I thought you were going to leave without me. Again.'

They looked at one another for a moment before stepping forward and embracing.

'Beal?'

'Mm?'

'Are you wiping your nose on my shoulder?' They laughed and moved apart.

'Yeah. Lovely. We need to get a shift on,' Fix pointed out.

Barb grabbed his torch and ran back to the room she'd been in. She gently shook Max as she held it above him. He looked terrible. Dried blood had spread across much of his face, and the wound still looked tender and liable to start bleeding again.

'Max? Can you get up?' Barb pulled him gently to a sitting position, and the movement unsettled him. He fell to his knees on the floor and was violently sick. Barb handed him the dried-blood shirt to wipe his mouth as he got unsteadily to his feet.

'Fix, you'll have to take him out and start getting him away. I'll go and get the kids.'

Fix started to protest until Barb grabbed him by the front of his shirt. 'If you want me to forget that you turned us in, you need to step up and do your bit now.' He nodded unhappily. 'Where are all the kids?'

'They're on the top floor.'

Barb stayed long enough to see that he was really heading out, supporting Max, before she ran for the stairs. She was grateful to see Beal behind her, watching as they quietly made their way up.

She knew this building so well after years of creeping around during the night and barrelling about during the day. But now it seemed creepy. There were none of the sounds of sleeping children as they muttered and turned in their beds. No whispered bickering or thuds of small bodies rolling off their mattresses. Just the echo of their overloud boots on the hard floors.

65

Finally, they reached the sixth floor and found children huddled together in the cramped rooms. It wasn't hard to wake them but considerably more difficult to stop them making too much noise. Barb cringed as the little ones started to wail as they pulled them up and tried to make their way to the fire escape on the third floor.

Luckily, Helen and Will were close to the door and knew all the remaining children.

As Barb started to lead them down the stairs, Mary came up and grasped her arm.

'I'm going back down to Shaw.'

Barb held her hand tight. 'No. No, we're on our way out. If you go down, we'll lose you.'

'I'm the distraction, remember? If I don't go, you probably won't get away.'

'But then *you* won't get away.'

'I don't want to. I want to stay with Shaw.'

'We won't be able to come looking for you. You can't go,' Barb said in frustration.

'Too late,' Mary laughed as she headed off. 'Stop panicking. I can look after myself. I want to stay with him.'

Barb stamped with frustration. Too bad. If she was going to act like an idiot, then she had to suffer the consequences. It was her or forty children, and right now, she liked the grouchy children a whole lot more than she liked Mary.

66

It wasn't the cries of the children that woke Shaw, but the sound of footsteps crossing the hall to the front door, quietly unlocking it and slipping out into the night.

Years of Wucker training had taught him to distinguish different people by the sound of their tread, and this was definitely not someone who he trusted to be leaving by this route in the middle of the night.

Mary was gone, but he wasn't really surprised.

He dressed quickly and took his pistol in his hand, ready for action.

Quietly he crossed the room and slid along the wall towards the entrance. He stopped as he saw the door slowly opening again and a slight figure slipping inside. They moved quietly across the floor, failing to see Shaw ready to leap.

As they passed him, Shaw grabbed the figure and swung them around heavily into the wall, winding them and making them mute.

'Who is out there?'

The figure fought for breath, swallowing and gasping until they finally felt oxygen coming back into their body.

'Your friends. They're your friends. I'm helping you.'

'So why didn't you think to tell me, Fix?'

'You were busy in there with that girl.' He tried to joke with Shaw but quickly saw that wasn't endearing him to the bigger man.

'They wanted to know if Barb or a strange girl had turned up. I was helping you, Shaw. They'll be happy with you again now they've got them. You will remember your friend Fix helped you get back in with them, won't you?'

Shaw pushed his face near Fix's. 'Oh, yes, I'll remember this, Fix. The trouble is, you won't want me to remember it.' He pushed him onto the ground. 'You're so ready to believe I want this girl dead. Barb was only too quick to assume I'd be happy to go after my brother. You all have such a low opinion of me and my motives.'

He pointed the gun towards Fix.

'You're a Wucker.'

'Yes. And you're a snitch that would sell his granny if it made him money.'

'My granny's dead,' Fix whimpered quietly.

'What sort of Wucker did you sell us to?'

'Don't know what you mean.'

'Yes, you do. Which ones, Fix?'

'Black Crow.'

Shaw's heart sank. The elite hit squad. Well, if he had to go down against the Black Crow, so be it. He hauled Fix up and dragged him to his office. Mary had gone from the bed in the back room, so he shoved Fix in and locked the door. He didn't expect it would hold him for long, but it should test his lock-picking skills and delay him for a bit.

He opened the drawer of the desk in the office and took

out a box of rounds, which he poured into his tunic pockets. The two shotguns they'd taken off Barb and her friends were leaned against the wall, and he grabbed them too.

He hadn't been lying when he'd told Barb that his child-hood memories had come flooding back when he'd returned to this place. Years of neglect and bullying here had ensured he'd found every nook and cranny in his attempts to stay hidden as a boy, and he doubted anyone knew the secret ways in and out as well as he did.

Back in the hall, he could hear the group making their way down to the third floor, where no doubt they would be leaving through the fire exit, into an open space and the waiting arms of the Black Crow. If they did that, they wouldn't live.

Shaw headed for the stairs and took them two at a time. There was no time to lose.

67

I t was slow going, and the group had only made it down two floors when they came across Max slumped on the stairs. Barb sobbed as she desperately felt his neck for a pulse and jumped as his hand came up to grab her.

'Barb, I'm sorry. Everything is moving. Leave me behind.'

'Don't be ridiculous. You have a concussion. Come on, we need to keep moving. Where's Fix?' *Stupid question*, she thought. *Fix is saving his own skin, as usual.*

Pulling Max up, the group moved off again.

While she was mad with Mary, she also hoped that she would manage to distract Shaw long enough to help them get away and fatally infect him into the bargain so they didn't have to worry about him coming after them ever again.

So when she literally ran into him on the stairs, she couldn't help screaming.

It was as if her shriek let loose all the fear that the younger children had been struggling to contain, and suddenly the ranks began to break. Some of them turned and tried to run back up the stairs, away from Shaw. Others lay on the floor and curled into small balls of misery.

'Stop!' He shouted in a clear, decisive voice.

The children froze, and there was a clear moment of silence brought on by surprise, fear or compliance.

He spoke quietly. 'There will be a prize for all those who can line up without a sound.'

At first they hesitated, and then gradually some began to move back into the line.

Barb looked at him defiantly. 'What's the prize? A night in the locked room?'

He gave her a cool look. 'A route out of here that takes you safely away from the Black Crow who are waiting to shoot you out the front.'

She shook her head. 'You're bluffing.'

'Your friend Fix found another way to make money, but it involved setting us all up.'

Barb looked around. 'Where is he? I'm going to kill him.'

Shaw raised an eyebrow. 'And you accuse me of being the violent one. Right, we need to move. I'll take you down to the exit. We're going through the boiler room in the basement and out through the back.'

Barb looked at him uncertainly.

'Stop worrying. It goes straight into the graveyard, and no one knows it's there. I used to use it to get out of this place when we lived here before.'

He handed Barb one of the shotguns and looked at the scared children behind her. 'You need to lead the way to the woods, but we need someone strong at the back. Where's your farmer?'

'He's at the back, but he has a bad concussion from

when someone bashed him on the head with a gun,' Barb shot back acidly.

Shaw looked sheepish. 'He needs to be further forward, then.'

He gave Barb one of the shotguns and pushed his way back through the children to Max. 'Take these little ones forward,' he said to him.

'No. I need to help.' Max staggered a little.

'You're needed at the front,' Shaw insisted.

He rearranged the younger ones further forward in the line, and finding Helen and Will, he pulled them to the back. 'You're the strongest in the pack,' he told them earnestly. 'You need to keep the back together and ensure they keep moving. You must not lose any of the children. This is the hardest part.'

He looked at the remaining shotgun and the two youngsters before him. Will shook slightly, but Helen returned his appraising stare without flinching. The shotgun was too long for either of them, so, reaching into his holster, he took out his revolver. 'Here, you might need this. Make sure you shoot the other Wuckers, not me.'

He gave a wry smile, then emptied the rounds out of his pockets into Will's. Quickly he showed Helen how to open the chamber and load it. Then, with a decisive movement, he handed it over, clasped her shoulder and looked into her worried face. 'You can do it. I know you can.'

Turning to Will, he said, 'Be her lookout. Count her shots, and keep her supplied with ammunition. You need to work as a team.'

He went back to the front of the line, and they moved off again with renewed energy. He indicated to the scared faces that they were to be quiet, and he led them down the remaining stairs, then past the ground floor into the basement through a small, dark door.

At the bottom, a dank corridor stretched beneath the Bank. A dim strip of low-energy bulbs made it just light enough to see their way to the other end. Before them lay a huge metal door, wide enough to go through in pairs – or to push a coffin through, as they used to do when it was a functioning hospital.

Shaw pulled out the keys once again and unlocked it. 'Even if they find this exit, it will take them a while to get through this.' He suddenly stopped. 'Where's Mary?'

Barb looked horrified. 'She went back to find you. She ... she wanted to stay here with you.'

Shaw felt as if he'd been punched in the stomach. 'I need to go back for her.'

Barb couldn't argue, but she also didn't think it was a search that would end well. She realised that this might be the last time she saw Shaw.

'There's something I need to tell you, Shaw.'

'Now's not really the moment. Tell me later.' He went to move away, but Barb grabbed the top of his sleeve.

'You have to listen. It's important.'

He looked at her impatiently. 'What?'

She pulled him down towards her, and she reached up to whisper in his ear.

He looked shocked as he stared at her, and she nodded. She took his hand.

'You'd better get moving. Go. I'll lock it behind you. Just keep going, and set the pace to these little ones at the front.'

He watched as Barb led them out.

As the last of the children passed through the door, she heard it shut behind them. She was aware of Max a little way back in the line, staggering about but keeping up.

About ten minutes out from the Bank, they heard shots that brought little squeaks of fear from the children. Barb turned and encouraged them to keep walking. Behind her she could hear Helen soothing and prodding the small group along. Whatever was happening back at the Bank, they needed to put as much distance as they could between them and it. She didn't fancy her group's chances against a well-armed professional team of Wuckers.

68

Once Shaw locked the door, he made his way back along the corridor and stopped at the bottom of the stairs. He leaned against the wall and took some deep breaths. His Wucker training had taught him to remain calm, to detach and assess the situation, to maximise the best response.

He was panicking.

Where was Mary? He had used the same main staircase but not passed her. Time was running out; they would storm the building soon. There would be ten elite fighters in a Black Crow unit, and they'd have spent some time fully assessing the building and its access points. His best hope was that they'd have ruled out the rear as too inaccessible or overgrown. Once he started shooting, it would probably be all over for him with ten against one. He had to use his advantage of knowing the building and his training with his hands and knife.

However, all this was pointless if he was searching for Mary or if they found her first.

He crept quickly up to the ground floor and peered carefully out into the hall. There was a little moonlight, and in it, he saw Mary standing in the doorway of his office. But he also saw the doorknob of the front door turning very, very slowly.

Quickly he ran across the floor, grabbing Mary's hand and pulling her to the stairs. Getting behind her, he grasped her waist and started propelling her up.

'Don't say anything. They're here,' he whispered.

She seemed to grasp the urgency of the situation and moved with him until they got to the first floor.

The Black Crows would be right behind them. As soon as they secured the hall, they would split up and start sweeping the floors one by one.

Shaw opened the door to the laundry room, and they went in. Indicating the huge washing machine, he helped Mary up into the drum and grabbed some sheets from the floor. Crumpling them up, he went to push them in front of her. 'Whatever you hear, stay put. I'll come back for you, but you must stay here and not make a sound. I promise I'll be back.'

She smiled and looked directly at him. 'I know.'

He tucked her in, arranged the sheets to cover her and gently pushed the door to, ensuring there was a crack in the door to let air in.

He was tempted to stay close to protect her, but he knew that he had to start picking off the Black Crows if they were to stand any chance of getting out.

69

Progress felt painfully slow as they travelled over the uneven terrain.

At the back, Helen kept scanning around her, sweeping the gun back and forth at every shadow. The only thing that kept her from shooting every passing tree was the fact that she was too terrified to pull the trigger.

Will kept them moving along, and steps became automatic, so she almost bumped into Max, who had fallen back behind the main body of the group.

As they moved further away from the Bank, Helen slowly began to relax, and the gun drooped in her hand, so she was startled when Max lunged forward and grabbed it suddenly from her.

Raising it up, Max shouted out, 'Down!' and Helen needed no further warning to fall to the ground. Two shots rang out, followed by a thud.

On the ground lay a body in a Wucker uniform.

Max got shakily to his feet, and they all stared at the bloody figure. Eventually, he walked over and, steeling himself, grabbed the sleeve of the nearest arm and pushed it up and over, rolling the body onto its back. Max had expected a man but it was a woman in black fatigues. He sprang away, but when she didn't move, he crawled back over and tentatively touched her. She was young, and dead.

Max went to pass the gun back to Helen, but she shook her head and held up her hands.

Max looked at the pale faces of the youngsters and nodded. Indicating to them to keep moving, he took up the rear point of the pack.

He turned to Helen. 'I'm feeling better. You go up the line and tell Barb to keep moving on.'

70

Shaw sped up the stairs to the top floor and hid himself several rooms in. He arranged a screen around the bed to make the searcher come right in to check the area, then moved back into the corner and the shadow of the cupboard. He stowed the shotgun in the corner and then he waited.

It wasn't long before he heard quiet steps. They paused and moved off in different directions along the corridor. He strained to hear them go into the room next door. Then it began. He watched the door swing quietly open, and a figure stepped through, moving towards the screen to pull it away. He lunged forward, using his knife to kill them with a swift stab to the neck. One down, nine to go.

The adrenaline pumped through him as he picked up the Crow's weapon and tucked it into his empty holster, leaving the bulky shotgun behind.

Mary drifted into his thoughts, and he forced the image back. If he lost focus, he would lose this fight. He listened carefully for the other Black Crow on this floor.

He made his way down the corridor, dodging between open doors, and managed to surprise the second one as he left a room. Again he managed a clean and quiet kill. The odds were becoming more favourable.

He knew that he couldn't risk slowing the pace now. Before long they would be expected to check in and confirm their area was clear, and once the reports failed to arrive, they would know something was wrong.

Shaw slipped down the stairs and took out two more Black Crows in quick succession. Only six more to go.

It had felt relatively easy so far, and Shaw began to relax a little, which was when it all started to go wrong.

As he turned into the third-floor corridor, he practically bumped into one of the Black Crows. They had a pistol in hand, and Shaw knocked their hand upwards to send the round above their heads and into the ceiling, where it lodged, sending a shower of plaster down on them. Twisting the Crow's wrist, Shaw wrenched the gun out of their hand and shot them before turning the gun to shoot the other Crow, who had come running out of a room further down.

He could already hear others coming up the stairs, so he ran for the fire escape, and throwing the door open, he flung himself out and slammed it behind him. He scrabbled for the keys and, with a shaking hand, pushed a key in and locked them in.

Almost immediately he heard shots being fired at the lock to release it, and he nearly tumbled down the outside steps as he rushed to get down. He leapt down the last stretch and hesitated for a second before running towards the wooded area.

Shots were fired behind him, and he felt a searing pain in his left arm as one of the Crows' rounds found him just as he reached the edge of the trees. He shut his mind to the agonising wound and pushed his way into the undergrowth. He needed to be able to maintain a distance in front of the pursuers to carry out his plan, so he frantically pulled at the brambles and ivy that snagged him. His hands bled as thorns pierced his skin, but eventually, he reached the low wall of the cemetery and was just a quick run from the outer door of the basement corridor, which the group had escaped through earlier.

He dodged and jumped over the headstones and swore as his ankle caught in a hole sunken into an old grave. Behind him he could hear bodies crashing through the undergrowth, more concerned with speed than stealth now they had their target nearly in sight.

He fumbled for the correct key, almost dropping them all, but once he found it, he unlocked the door to the corridor and flung it open. Then, pushing on through the vegetation, he looked for a tree he could climb.

In normal circumstances, in normal times, he could climb any tree, however tall or daunting. With his left arm hanging almost useless and hands ripped and bleeding, he knew it had to be a simple climb. All the trees had had years to stretch and grow, so it seemed he would never find one with a low branch, but finally he found a smaller tree, and he struggled to pull himself up with his one good arm, all the time praying that no one caught him at this vulnerable moment.

Once he was high enough, he steadied himself and got his gun ready. He felt dizzy and could feel the blood trickling down his arm. He was barely ready before three Crows came battering through the undergrowth after him and, looking across the graveyard, saw the open door. They slowed and split up, approaching it from different directions before stopping by the door for a moment. It was obvious who was in charge, as orders were exchanged, sending one Crow in through the entrance of the basement, and another further on into the undergrowth to look for Shaw. The officer stood at the door, scanning the area and taking stock of the situation.

Shaw saw the officer lift his head to search the trees, and he knew that within the next few seconds, he would be in his sight line, but the man walking towards him was not near enough to jump on, as he'd planned. As the officer spotted him and raised his gun, Shaw leapt down, using the nearest Crow as a shield against the officer's shot.

Shaw looked the surprised Crow in the face and then shot him before springing to his right. He banked on the officer expecting him to stay put or go left towards a standing gravestone, and his luck held as the shot went wide, and he rolled, fighting the agony of his injured arm, knelt up, took aim and shot the officer. He had been a crack shot in the Wuckers, with every chance of promotion to the Crows himself. It showed as the officer crumpled and fell.

Shaw staggered forward to the door, ensuring he stood to the side rather than giving the Crow inside a perfect silhouette to aim for.

He listened.

Inside he heard footsteps heading back to the door, which suddenly slid to a stop. There were a few hesitant steps.

'Sir?' a woman's voice called out.

Shaw remained silent.

A few more steps echoed off the concrete. Then the Crow turned and ran away from the door and back into the building.

Shaw leaned against the wall for a few moments, trying to decide which way to enter the building. There were two Crows left, which were good odds, but he was injured.

One Crow in the hallway could be covering both the

front door and the stairs up from this corridor. The other could watch the fire escape on the third floor. He needed another way in, and he could only think of one other option.

As he gathered his thoughts and made his plans, he heard a rustling sound approaching quickly from behind. There was no time to stand. He rolled onto his front, pointing his gun towards whoever was heading towards him, but while he could hear movement, there was no sign of a person. Whatever it was, it was now upon him and burst out into the open directly towards him before swerving to avoid a head-on collision.

He shot high to miss the wild pig that flew towards him, and dropped his head shakily onto his arms. He smelt the leaves and soil beneath him and laughed hysterically.

He calmed himself. It was not over yet. As he sat up, he saw the pig rooting around near the door, and a thought occurred to him.

Two more Crows to go. Perhaps Crows could be as spooked by pigs as he had been.

71

Mary soon found that it was extremely uncomfortable in the giant washing machine.

For one thing, the surface was hard and unforgiving, with high ridges to catch and toss the washing. For another, it was full of holes, which wasn't a problem at the start, but after a short while, they began to cut into her, printing rows of raised circles across her skin.

She found trying to shift made the drum rock back and forth, only making the situation worse, as it made her feel seasick and anxious that she wouldn't be able to make it still again.

It wasn't long, however, before she heard steps, and the door to the laundry opened.

She put her hands over her mouth to stop herself calling out to Shaw. If it was him, he would know where to find her. If it wasn't, she didn't want to be found.

The feet came to the machines and moved along the row.

The door opened.

The long metal nose of a gun prodded the sheets, and Mary tried to shrink back under the pressure and do her best impression of dirty washing. The gun went back out, and she held her breath. Was the person convinced?

In the distance, there was the sound of shots, and the searcher suddenly turned to go, slamming the washing machine door as they went.

She waited until she could be sure the Crow had left, and then tentatively she put out a hand to push the door open a little.

It wouldn't move. There was no longer a careful chink for air, and when Mary pushed the door, it was tightly locked and sealed. Mary breathed deeply, trying not to panic.

Already the temperature in the closed machine was rising, and water droplets were collecting on the glass.

She was trapped inside the machine, and it occurred to her that her only hope was that Shaw would be successful and not go and die, because he was the only person who knew she was there.

There were symbols that she had seen back at the Facility. She could only reliably remember the first. She took her finger and drew it in the condensation – M.

72

When Shaw had been little, he had sometimes resorted to climbing out through the small, high window in the toilets. Back then the height had been the problem; now it was the smallness.

There were other windows on the ground floor, but they would need to be smashed open, which would be noisy, and this one had been missing the glass for many years now. Also, he was pretty sure the Crows wouldn't be waiting for him in the toilet.

Of course, there was a good reason for that. They would look at that window and assume he wouldn't manage to get through it. They might well be right.

He wondered whether it would be better to go feet or head first. He didn't fancy landing head first in the loos, but there was nowhere to hold on to slot his feet in.

He held his gun out in case he needed it mid-climb and posted his arms through as if diving through the window. His head and shoulders followed through without too much trouble, and for a few seconds, he hung in the frame, catching his breath with his head dangling inside the toilets and his feet hanging down the outside wall.

This made his arm bleed more intensely, and the blood was rushing to his head, making him dizzy. With a huge effort, he used his good arm to push back and get his hips through the window. He let himself drop to the floor and lay there catching his breath.

The smell of urine was strong in the grout lines, which was enough incentive to make him get up and move.

He crouched near the door, resting his ear near the gap, trying to hear any clues that would help him locate the final two Crows.

Nothing.

He checked his gun was fully loaded, and that his knife was still tucked into his waistband. He wondered about trying to tie up the wound in his arm, but he just wanted to get this over with. He could sort it out later.

He was counting on one of the Crows being near the stairwell, watching for him coming in through either the basement corridor or the front door.

He closed his eyes and visualised the layout of the hallway.

73

L ying still in the washing drum really didn't seem so hard any more. In fact, the thought of moving sounded much more difficult.

Mary felt for her pulse but found it surprisingly hard to find and measure. It was weak and slow, like the rest of her.

Her mind went back to the room at the Facility, when sometimes she'd been able to switch off her functions and go into a dormant phase. This was where she went now.

Her brain was still ticking along, and without effort, Vander's face came to the front of her mind. His face was wider than Shaw's but had the same blue eyes. He was worried, less confident and sure than Shaw was. Poor Vander. He'd always been worried about her, trying to fix her.

She thought of Beal. Had she got away with Barb? Maybe if she'd had a sister in the Facility, she would have been happy to stay there. They could have talked and played and been friends.

She tried to think of Max and Frank. Frank was clearer. She wanted to see Frank again.

A tear slid down her cheek and was absorbed by the washing that was becoming her winding sheet.

'Shaw,' she whispered.

Where was Shaw? More than anyone else, she wanted to see Shaw.

74

As Shaw sat with his eyes closed, he heard a noise that made him smile. It was a clattering accompanied by an echoing squeal.

He used the cover of the gathering noise to risk looking out of the doorway. Sure enough, there was a dark figure there, warily backing out of the stairwell, which was amplifying the clamour.

The pig that Shaw had met in the graveyard, and then coaxed through the door, had finally found its way along the corridor and was now making its way up the stairs to the confusion of the Crow, who had no idea what was coming.

She fired off a couple of rounds, but like Shaw, thought the target was taller than it was, so they went harmlessly over the top of the pig, which was now hurtling up the stairs, screeching as it leapt up each step.

Shaw stealthily moved towards the Crow from behind and was about to stab her, as he had the others, when she stepped back and slipped, falling and avoiding the knife. Realising that the real danger was behind her, the Crow raised her gun to shoot Shaw, who leapt forward and grabbed her hands. He swung his body around so the shot went past him, and tried to loosen the Crow's grip on the gun.

The pig finally escaped the stairwell and, finding itself trapped in the hallway, ran around them and then between their legs, tripping them and sending them both to the ground, where they landed with a force that winded them both.

Shaw caught his breath first and fumbled for the gun, but the Crow wasn't far behind him, and they grappled as each tried to get the winning grip, wrestling on the floor. Swinging his foot around, Shaw kicked his attacker in the shin and used the momentary shock to pull the gun away. With a final flash of focus, he aimed and shot the Crow dead.

He pulled his trapped leg from under the body and scrambled backwards towards the shadow of the doorway. He listened between each heaving gulp to check if all the noise had drawn the attention of the final Crow, but if it had, they were approaching quietly.

Now it was just the two of them.

75

Shaw squatted with his back against the door frame as he regulated his breathing and checked the chamber of the gun. Two rounds left. He would need to make sure they really counted.

He took a bandage from the stockroom and tied it tightly around his arm. It wasn't clean or tidy, but it would hopefully stop him leaving a trail of blood for the final Crow to follow.

He was itching to go and check on Mary, but he had to deal with the final Crow before it was safe to.

There was only one option: to sweep the building from the top.

He wasn't looking forward to this. He slipped off his boots and tucked them behind the door, then started to move silently up the stairwell.

76

Mary was floating in a multicoloured sea of despair.

She tried to grab each colour in turn and hold it in her hands, but each time she closed her fist, the colour evaporated into wisps of smoke.

Red was gone.

Yellow was gone.

Green was gone.

Blue was gone.

Now there was only white. Surrounding her. Closing in on her. Pressing down and squeezing the life out of her.

77

The top three floors were clear.

It had taken more time than he'd have liked, but Shaw had searched them thoroughly.

The second and third floors would be easier, as they were emptier and had less furniture to hide inside or behind. But then that meant he would also be out in the open.

He decided that he would check Mary was all right once he got to the first floor, while going past. He had to check the laundry room anyway.

78

M ary thought about holding Shaw and was glad it was her last thought.

79

He'd made it to the first floor with no sign of anyone other than the Crows he'd already killed, and they remained untouched and unmoved. It had given him a chance to get more ammunition.

He hesitated at the laundry door with his hand on the handle. Removing it, he decided it would be better to check the rest of this floor first rather than be distracted by Mary and have them creep up on him at this stage.

80

Shaw had said to get into the drum.

Mary giggled.

A drum.

She knew that word.

Vander had kept tapping things.

He'd said everything could be a drum.

She could hear thumping. Was it her heart or a drum?

D-rum.

D-rum.

D-rum.

D.

D.

D.

...

81

The first floor was checked and clear apart from the laundry. As Shaw entered the room, he saw Mary's pale white hand pressed against the glass of the washing machine door and froze.

He dropped his gun and grappled with the door latch, trying to force it, then angrily struggling to work the mechanism correctly.

Finally, he managed it, and as he opened the door, her arm dropped lifelessly out.

He pulled out the sheets to get to her and then gently lifted her down onto the floor.

'Mary. Mary,' he whispered frantically.

Her lips were blue and her skin almost translucent. Shaw pushed back her head and started desperately blowing his life into her. He counted the breaths through his tears and the anger.

He wanted her back. He needed her back.

It had been a long time since he'd really wanted anyone.

He had wanted his mother after she'd died of the Red Plague.

He had wanted his father after he'd got squashed while clearing the old houses for the Danssy Corporation.

He'd wanted a big brother. He had wanted Vander.

Now he wanted Mary, and this time, he wasn't going to give up.

His arms ached from pumping her chest, and for a moment, he was alarmed to see blood speckling her top. Then he realised it was his, from his wounded arm. He tasted the salt of his tears when he opened his mouth and bent to press his lips to hers. He blew into her, watching her chest rise before resuming the compressions. He worked on until finally, as he sat back on his heels, he could see the colour returning to her face and that she was now breathing on her own.

He knew he had done damage to her in his efforts to bring her back and didn't dare lift her, in case a broken rib punctured something more critical. Crossing to the shelves, he got down armfuls of clean linen and brought it back to cushion her head and cover her.

He had no idea how much time had passed, but now the fear of discovery overwhelmed him. All the searching had been in vain, as the final Crow was still alive and could now be anywhere in the building. The only good point was that they hadn't burst in on them while he'd been resuscitating Mary. Otherwise, it would all have been over.

He sat beside her on the floor and carefully watched her chest rise and fall, rise and fall, rise and fall. Taking a towel, he wiped his face and stood to go and find the final Crow.

He pulled the door quietly shut behind him and took the key. Should he lock her in? His attempts to keep her alive would be wasted if she died of dehydration or starvation because she couldn't get out. He felt sick at how close he had come to losing her.

82

It was many hours later, as the sun rose high in the sky, when Frank saw the straggly pack stagger up the road to the farm. The smallest children were too exhausted to cry, and almost too exhausted to stand, as he led them into the temporary beds he'd made up in the barn. He wasn't ashamed to shed a few tears as he saw Max turn the corner, bringing up the end of the group, and he had to prise the gun out of his hand before sending him to bed and taking up his position at the bottom of the road, watching for anyone following or trying to attack. The shotguns seemed to have disappeared, but now was not the time to try to make sense of it all.

It was a while before he gathered his thoughts and realised that Mary hadn't been in the group, and his initial elation over Max began to fade a little.

83

Shaw moved around the Bank, becoming less careful and more frantic at every turn.

Where was that Crow?

He risked going out and scouting around too, but still there was no sign of them.

Uneasily he came back in and locked the door. It was not protocol to return without the rest of the team, but maybe they had a newer team member, who had got spooked. Either way, it would not be long before base came looking for them. They wouldn't let a team of Crows just disappear.

He collected some food and a bottle of water from his office and made his way up to the laundry room.

Mary was lying where he had left her, with her eyes wide open and her teeth clenched. He came in quickly and took her hand and stroked her hair. She made a small whimper and held on to him tightly.

'You'd stopped breathing. I had to do CPR, and I've probably broken at least one rib. I'm sorry.'

She opened her eyes and made a small movement with

her lips that could have been an attempt at a smile or could have been a grimace.

He was wondering what to tell her when she gasped out, 'Where are the others?'

'The children have gone. Hopefully, they are away safely with your friends. The Wuckers ... the Wuckers are mostly dead.'

'Mostly?'

'One unaccounted for.'

She nodded. 'What now?'

'We should find somewhere safer to hide, but then rest a bit. Give you a chance to start healing.'

'Where?'

Shaw thought. He didn't know where the farm was, or even if it was near enough to get to.

'Best start out in the woods,' he decided. It would be hard to search it during the night and would at least give them a chance of getting away.

He helped her up off the floor and persuaded her to take some sips of water and a small bite of food. Slowly they made their way to the stairs and down to the ground floor. He wanted to scoop her up and carry her, both to speed things up and to make it easier for her, but he was worried about causing more damage.

Finally, they entered the woods.

Mary's thoughts immediately flew back to that night when she had stumbled through the trees, supported by Vander, and she started to cry.

'We're nearly there,' Shaw soothed, assuming it was the pain that was affecting her.

As soon as he was confident they had enough distance between them and the Bank, he helped her sit and started arranging some branches to lean against.

'I'm going back for some supplies.'

'No.' She held on to his arm, terrified of being left alone in the dark.

He prised her fingers gently off his sleeve and squeezed her hand reassuringly. 'I won't be long. We need some warm things and food.'

He made his way back carefully, being sure to lay marks he would recognise to be able to find her again. Once in he went to the storeroom to collect some food and scratchy blankets.

A crashing sound behind him made him leap around and drop it all. He raised his gun and shuffled forward, easing around the shelf unit. There was nothing except a bowl rolling across the floor.

His heart was pounding. He did not want to lose out now. Righteous indignation flared up in him. He was not going to go down now to a Crow who was hiding in the shadows.

'Come on, then,' he hissed.

He stepped back and then threw all his weight into his shoulder, which careened into the unit. It wobbled as if unsure whether to topple, and with another push, it tilted past its tipping point and thundered over, taking the next set with it like a row of giant dominoes. Shaw leapt out ready to shoot at anyone escaping from the crush, but instead of a human, a small pig came screaming out from under the piles of tins and split bags.

He laughed with relief, jumped at the echo of his own laugh and took a deep breath.

He counted out ten clear minutes in silence, straining his ears for any slight indication that the commotion had brought the last Crow out of their hiding spot, but there was nothing.

Surely they would have come out after that?

He had an uneasy thought that the Crows often had a tactic of sending an outlier to scout the area. *What if they met Barb's group? What if they were still out there?*

He couldn't help the children now, but he should get back to Mary.

He took a detour as he left the building, entering the woods too far over and crouching down to watch for anyone following or observing him. When he was confident that there was no one about, he zigzagged through the trees, setting up a few wrong trails before finally taking the correct route and heading back to Mary.

84

As they lay next to one another, sharing their body heat, Mary spoke up.

'Talk to me.'

'What about?'

'Anything. Anything to take my mind off the pain. Tell me about your mother.'

Shaw thought for a moment. 'I don't really remember her,' he admitted. 'I was only three years old when she died of the plague. Vander was older. She'd been looking after him since his father died in an earlier outbreak. She met my dad, and they got together and had me. We only had three years together as a family. Then it all fell apart.'

He thought about how jealous he'd been of Vander for having their mother for so much longer. He'd had a chance to know her.

'Then your father got ill too.'

'He didn't get ill. He died in an accident. He was squashed when a building collapsed. They pulled him out, but he was too badly injured. He held on for a few weeks ...' Shaw realised this was the first time he had ever talked to anyone about his father. Now he'd started, it seemed impossible to stop.

'He never wanted to put Vander in the Bank,' he said softly. 'He'd promised our mother that he wouldn't, but he couldn't manage two little kids on his own. There wasn't enough money or food. He was working every shift he could to raise enough money to buy him back out, but every time he tried, the price had gone up. He shouldn't have been working when the accident happened, but he was doing an extra shift again. He should have been safely at home with me. When he died, he said, "At least you will be with Vander now. He'll look after you."'

'He must have been glad to be back together.'

'No, not at all. He made me promise not to talk about it. I don't blame him. He got sent away. Why would he want a little brother hanging around him? Especially the one that had got chosen over him. We didn't want him before but expected him to step up when it suited us. Probably for the best. He'd have to have gone back to the Bank anyway when Dad died.'

Mary squeezed his arm, and they both lay quietly for a while.

'Vander told me no one ever loved him,' Mary said at last.

'I guess that's what he believed, but it wasn't true.'

Eventually, Shaw felt Mary's body go heavy as she drifted off to sleep, and was reassured to feel her breathing in and out. He was wide awake. He was tempted to slip once more into the past now that Mary had opened the door, but it was easier to think about the future than the past. In the morning, they needed to move again, but he was conflicted about what that would mean.

What he wanted to do was to pack up and head a long,

long way away. Head off into the unknown, just him and Mary. Whatever was out there couldn't be worse than here.

But Mary wouldn't be able to travel far, and once the Wuckers found the mess at the Bank, they would want to get whoever was responsible. If he disappeared, they would keep hunting until they found someone, which would probably mean they'd find the farm and the kids. He doubted they would think the kids were responsible, but by then they wouldn't really care; they'd have their scapegoats.

He rolled his eyes at himself – what a time to grow a conscience. But there was something else too. When they had met, Mary had seen him more clearly than anyone else. And he had seen her too.

Mary stirred and, wincing slightly, leaned in against him.

'Did you ever know your mother?' he asked her.

She thought for a moment. 'Not really.'

He let her think for a moment.

'I met a woman from the Facility who was sort of my mother. She said I'm her clone.'

She lifted her head to make sure that Shaw was listening, and he smiled to encourage her.

'If she was my mother, she wouldn't have done those horrible things to me though, would she?'

'Sometimes people do bad things to those they care about.' Shaw stroked her hair. 'Mary?'

'Mm?'

'Were you with Vander when he died?'

She lay very still with her head on his chest, listening to his heart beating steadily.

'I was with him in the flats and when we escaped from there.'

Shaw nodded. He remembered leading his squad in. He

thought of how carefully he had picked the worst and least experienced recruits to go with him and how easy it had been to misdirect them so they allowed his brother to slip through their fingers.

'What then?'

'We went to the river, and he went looking for something. I thought he was looking for Scratch. He told me to stay there, but he never came back.'

'You met Scratch?'

'He brought us food in the flat.'

Shaw stroked her hair as he thought. 'So you went to the hall?'

'I met Cress and Beal, and they took me home.'

The light was starting to break through the leaves above them, and a light mist was rising off the ground.

'They said there was a floater and it was Vander. They said he was dead, but I never saw him.'

'Where did you meet him?'

'In the Facility. It was where I lived. I was a prisoner there, and he rescued me. I came with him and lived with him for a bit, but he got sick, and then he went in the river.'

'Why did he get sick?' Shaw asked, although he felt quite sure he knew the answer.

Mary didn't reply.

'Mary, do you realise everyone you live with gets sick?' he asked gently.

'Max and Barb aren't sick. You're not sick.'

'I guess we probably have some immunity,' Shaw mused out loud. 'A lot of the kids didn't though. When the sickness came back, a lot of the kids died.'

Mary lay very still. Then, in a small voice, she said, 'I was never here. It wasn't anything to do with me.'

'Scratch was though.'

'It wasn't me!' Mary started to struggle to get up, but Shaw put his arms around her. 'It's okay. It's okay. I'm just thinking that if we want to stay together, perhaps we should think of finding somewhere away from other people.'

'You want to put me back in the Facility?' She pulled away again, angry and afraid.

'No.' He caught her hand. 'I promise I won't do that.'

'I'm not going back there,' she stated. 'But I'm not living alone either. Why should I? I want to go and live on the farm like everyone else.'

'Even if it makes them ill?'

She looked at him defiantly. 'It won't. It's not my fault.'

Shaw nodded gravely. He wouldn't lock her up, but how could he let her keep killing so many people? He had no doubt she was the source of all the outbreaks.

'We could go somewhere, just us together.'

'I want to see Frank again, and Max. I want to see Barb too.'

Shaw thought of Barb standing in the doorway, whispering in his ear. He thought of the fluttering kick he had felt as she took his hand and pressed it to her stomach.

He couldn't let Mary keep infecting everyone.

Vander had set all this in motion, and it looked like it might be up to him to bring it to a close.

He had a plan.

It wasn't a good plan, but he did have one.

85

Frank found the trail the children had taken to the farm. It was fairly easy to follow in the day, as the little convoy had trampled their way between the trees, squashing the vegetation and breaking branches in their flight from the Bank. Occasionally he found a toy or a piece of clothing that confirmed that he was on the right track.

Barb and Max had wanted to go instead, or at least to go with him, but he had promised to go slowly and not to do anything dangerous.

'I'm just going to look, see what I can find out. The kids need you here to organise them,' he pointed out. 'That looks a lot harder to me than a day trip in the woods.'

He practically tripped over the dead Wucker, her uniform blending with the forest floor. Only a youngster. What a waste. Will had told him what had happened, and it made him sad but relieved.

Passing through a dense patch of trees, he caught sight of the edge of Mary's yellow cardigan and would have called out, but even the slow walk had robbed him of enough breath to summon up a shout.

She was with someone, a man. Frank got the gun ready to defend her or himself.

As Frank drew nearer, he saw the man help her gently to her feet. She seemed injured, but her companion was supporting her. Was he that Shaw character? He didn't look mean. In fact, they looked like a happy couple out for a walk. The man leaned towards her and whispered a comment in her ear. Then, reaching down, he picked up a vibrant red leaf and presented it to her, which made her laugh. Frank retreated behind a tree, embarrassed to be intruding as he saw them draw together.

He prepared himself to act surprised, thinking they would turn towards him and meet him on the path towards the farm, but after a few moments, it became clear they weren't heading this way. He risked a quick peek from his hiding place and saw they were going back towards the Bank.

Surely not. Why weren't they coming to join the rest of the group?

He decided to follow them and check that Mary wanted to stay here. He started to walk but was stopped by the sound of heavy trucks pulling up on the gravel drive at the front of the Bank, and the crunch of big boots jumping out.

He expected Mary and the man to stop and duck down out of sight, but they carried on as if they hadn't heard. Frank wanted to warn them, to call out, but he was gripped by a pain in his chest. They must have heard. They must know that they were heading straight towards the danger.

Mary seemed to hesitate, but her friend said something to her that must have been reassuring, and they continued on. Before they stepped out of the woods, they stood together once more, and again they held each other. The man wrapped his arms around her, holding her close, and

Mary raised her face up. He cupped her cheek with his hand and kissed her, and Frank closed his eyes, transported to a moment when he was young, and Thea and he had been alone in the world, just needing to feel the press of another person to prove that they were still alive.

S haw wondered if he had ever felt this calm or certain before. Life suddenly seemed very simple. He guessed it had once felt this way in the arms of his mother as a baby, when life happened to you and your thoughts and needs were basic. Now he was happy because he had given up all the complications, and all that was left was taking comfort in doing what was right.

87

It all happened so suddenly. Barely had Frank opened his eyes when the man moved forward with Mary still in his arms, into the sun beyond the fringes of the trees, into the mass of Wuckers that lay beyond them.

Holding Mary tight with one arm, Shaw pulled a gun with the other, aimed high and shot over the head of the Wuckers.

There were shouts and threats. Then return shots rang out, and Mary and Shaw fell to the ground.

Frank's legs crumpled, and he slid down the tree.

His chest felt as if it were about to burst open as pain exploded in him. He pressed his face to the rough bark of the tree, feeling the ridges branding his face with new lines. He pressed until it hurt, to distract him from the pain in his chest.

Through a haze of pain, Frank watched the Wuckers go into the Bank and start bringing out the bodies of their comrades. They were all loaded onto a truck, and finally they went over to Shaw and Mary. A couple of figures shrouded in protective clothing brought over a body bag. There seemed to be a lot of debate and gesticulating about there being one bag and two bodies, but eventually, they squeezed both Mary and Shaw into it and zipped it up. It took four of them then to lift the bag and put it into a different van before bringing out a large bottle of liquid and sloshing it around over the gravel where they had lain.

Once they were done, they all clambered back into the trucks and drove off in a haze of dust. Gradually the strength returned to Frank's legs, and the pain in his heart became more of an ache. He was cold and stiff, but he forced himself to get up off the ground.

If he hadn't known that Max and Barb would come looking for him, he thought he might have lain down and died on the spot, but they would, so he wouldn't.

He turned his weary feet and retraced his steps to the farm.

89

L ying on her back, Barb could see only blue.

There was not a single cloud. She scanned the expanse above her, tracking the swirls of colour as the deep blue at the edges gradually bleached as it plunged into the blaze of the sun.

As she brushed her hands over the tips of the grass blades, they tickled her palms, and she could feel the buds of purple clover.

Barb rolled onto her side to gaze at her child, Zera, peacefully sleeping, wrapped in a soft yellow blanket that Helen had knitted for her.

This baby was the darling of the whole community, especially of auntie Beal and grandfather Frank.

Once Beal was fit, she had been back into the city and found some of her old group trying to scrape a living on the streets in ones or twos. Barb had wondered if she would come back, as they had good days and bad days trying to become sisters again. But Beal had persuaded some of her old friends to return with her, and they had moved into the upper house.

There could be friction when objects from Frank's

house vanished and rematerialised in High Brow, and every now and again, Frank would stomp up and reclaim anything he felt strongly about and ignore the things that didn't matter.

The kids slipped between the houses as the mood took them, and as long as designated crews arrived to do the jobs on the farm, it was all working surprisingly well with Barb in charge of Low Fell and Beal running High Brow.

Zera woke and kicked off the blanket. Barb leaned over to stroke her face and gaze into those beautiful blue eyes.

The
Charris
Facility

MEMORANDUM

Re: Microbe Ambassador Receptacle Y. (M.A.R.Y.)

- Recent theft and exposure of M.A.R.Y. has prompted a review of storage of all Microbe Ambassadors.
- New procedures require that all receptacles be kept in a permanent state of sedation.
- Receptacles will be maintained through intravenous feeds rather than meals, which will minimise human contact.
- This will apply to all receptacles A–X with immediate effect.

ACKNOWLEDGMENTS

When I set out to write about a post-pandemic dystopian world, the plan was to just visualise it, not to live it. I was happy to delve into the past, throw in some imagination and write a *fictional* story.

But the spirits of time decided to mix things up a bit. Sue and Rachel Bloomer had given me their comments and Leonora Bulbeck had just returned her excellent edits at the end of 2019, when we were thrown into the reality of a very real new contagion that would change all our priorities.

It took eight months, and the ever calm, clear and collected support of Katie Sadler, to make me go back and address the edits and reconnect with my characters and their story. I'm not sure if, or when, it would have happened otherwise.

I reread my script with trepidation — my perspective had shifted, but the story stood.

With the support and expertise of Rachael Mortimer, who proofread and gave invaluable feedback, and Rachel Lawston who designed a wonderful cover, it was ready to go!

I have been so fortunate to work with all these fabulous people, whose knowledge and professional skills elevated this book beyond anything I could have done without them.

Pre-pandemic, during the long writing process, my friend, Margaret Ring, listened to my many tangental thoughts on our laps around the Common — a combination of rambling and running.

Then there is my long-suffering family who have endured the distraction of a writer whose brain is in their book, rather than the real world. They have answered strange questions, given opinions (even if they were often thrown back in their faces, and then on calm reflection used anyway), and submitted to demands to 'just read this bit quickly' then handed fifty pages of script in the middle of their meal. Sean, Sam, Danny and Freddie have all lived through writing this book, especially as lockdown brought us all back into the home much more than would have happened otherwise.

My mother, Sue, spent a very, very large number of hours on the phone giving long-distance feedback at each stage. All writers should have someone they can call and talk about the merits of individual words in a sentence, and I am lucky to have a mum that fits that criteria.

I owe a huge debt of gratitude to every one of you mentioned above, for making this book happen.

Thank you.

ABOUT THE AUTHOR

When she was young Kate promised she would never go out with a boy called Sean (they were too naughty), study history (it was too boring) or be a teacher (too hard).

Luckily promises are made to be broken.

She now writes books inspired by fascinating stories from history, visits schools, using her ten years teaching experience, and is married to historian Sean Cunningham.

After all, life would be very boring if you knew how it was going to turn out.

Find out more about Kate and her books on www.readingriddle.co.uk

facebook.com/readingriddle

twitter.com/reading_riddle

instagram.com/reading_riddle

Lightning Source UK Ltd.
Milton Keynes UK
UKHW042145120422
401483UK00002B/277